THE
MAGICIAN'S
GIRL

THE MAGICIAN'S GIRL

DORIS GRUMBACH

W. W. NORTON & COMPANY

NEW YORK · LONDON

Copyright © 1987 by Doris Grumbach

First published as a Norton paperback 1993

Library of Congress Cataloging-in-Publication Data
Grumbach, Doris.   The magician's girl.
I. Title.
PS3557.R83M3   1993   813'.54—dc20   93-5782 CIP

ISBN: 978-0-393-31091-7

Grateful acknowledgment is made to Harper & Row, Publishers, Inc., for
permission to reprint a line from "The Bee Meeting" from *The Collected
Poems of Sylvia Plath,* edited by Ted Hughes. Copyright © 1963 by Ted Hughes.

W. W. Norton & Company, Inc.
500 Fifth Avenue, New York, N.Y. 10110
W. W. Norton & Company Ltd.
10 Coptic Street, London WC1A 1PU

Designed by Mary Cregan

For Gustave Flaubert, who wrote to his mistress in 1853: 'Everything one invents is true, you may be sure.'

And for William Kennedy, who taught me, through Francis Phelan in *Ironweed*, that 'every stinkin' damn thing you can think of is true.'

PART ONE

I am the magician's girl who does not flinch.

—SYLVIA PLATH

In these pages I have put down what I know for certain about Minna Grant's placid and only occasionally traumatic early life, her edenic college years, the cool ellipsis between the beginning of her marriage and its curiously uneventful end, and the sweet conclusion to the few climactic months she spent in the heartland. There remains much I can only guess at. Every life is a mystery, a 'real' one even more than a fictional one, one's own perhaps the greatest mystery. With all the solid evidence provided by diaries, letters, testimonies, confessions and memories, there is, at the core of a life history, an inscrutable enigma no biographer, friend or novelist can solve. We are left with the facts, softened and made more acceptable (and yes, believable) by charitable conjecture and the application of the imagination. So we make inspired guesses. That is all we have. That is what you will read here.

∽

MINNA GRANT'S FIRST MEMORY, at five, was of terror. At two o'clock Christmas morning she woke to see, in the gray-black light of a New York City apartment-house courtyard that defined her bedroom window, a great human shadow. The figure's hair seemed to spring out of its head; its face was blank in the darkness. Minna saw only the torso with sloping shoulders and enormous hips. There were no legs. She sat up rigid in bed and screamed. The sleeping warmth of her beloved bed, a crib mattress now mounted on a frame 'for a big girl,' her mother told her, had turned to ice at her legs. Her eyes, ears and nose felt as if they had been blown out, like tires, as if they had exploded while she screamed again and again. She thought her fear of the penumbral person in the window was emptying her head through all its holes.

'Wake up, wake up,' her mother said, shaking her. Minna *was* awake, had been awake all along, she believed, when the person appeared in the window, she wanted to tell her mother. But her mouth felt stuffed with her wet, swollen tongue. Her mother turned on the light: in the chandelier the five bare bulbs in their tulip holders lit up.

Her mother wrapped her in her arms. In the dissolving warmth of her mother's milk-dough breasts, Minna abandoned her terror. She breathed in the fragrance of her mother's bed-warm skin. 'I saw someone,' she said into the envelope of her mother's sheltering bosom.   'Not a soul is here,' her mother said, 'but me.'   Minna lifted her head and pointed. 'In the window.' But now in the light she saw a doll seated there, huge and curly-haired, its frilled dress filling the frame, its painted china face smiling maliciously as if it were in on the deception. The blue eyes looked amused at Minna's terror.

'It's your present. We put it in your room so you would find it first thing when you woke up. It's not a person. It's a present. Don't be frightened, dear. I'll take it away and put it under the tree. We made a mistake. Go to sleep, my love. Everything will be all right now.' She kissed Minna, turned out the light and left her wrapped in her quilt and covered with her mother's perfume and powder. 'Don't be afraid,' Minna said to herself. When she was able to look again she saw the person doll was gone, the window space restored to blank gray. Her mother had taken the Christmas present with her to the dining room, she thought. Minna slipped into comforting sleep.

To her parent's disappointment, she never played with

4

her Christmas doll. She kept her wrapped in an old diaper—dusting cloth at the back of her closet, 'to keep her clean,' she told her mother.

It was spring. Minna was six, in the first grade of Public School 9. To her, the city of New York was still a high gray fortress bound together inexplicably by strips of colorless sky. On one side of the fortress ran a long, shining river she could only see sections of, the part between streets that seemed to jut into it. It was Saturday. Her mother, a beautiful woman with a mouth so tight and small it looked disappointed and stern, and blue eyes like tidewater pools, always took her to the stores on Saturday. 'Let's go marketing,' her mother would say.   'I don't feel like it,' Minna usually replied. She had heard the sentence somewhere and thought of it as a proper grown-up response to all suggestions made to her.

Her mother said nothing but took her hand and held it while they waited in the hall for the elevator. The elevator 'boy' in his faded brown uniform, in service to 130 West Eighty-sixth Street for twenty-five years, always said, 'Morning to you, ma'am,' whatever time it was that he brought the clattering cage to the second floor and opened the wire door. 'Morning,' her mother said. They went down in silence. Still held by her mother's hand, resenting having to go marketing, Minna watched while her mother looked down at the sorted mail on the wide scarred table in the lobby. Rarely did her mother take one to open and read while they stood there. Even then, Minna knew her mother hoped for a letter with an odd stamp on it. Such a soft, thin letter came only, she believed, at Christmas and Easter.

They walked to Amsterdam Avenue, where her mother did most of her marketing. Sometimes Minna would ask to wait outside the store next to the carriages and their burdens of doll-babies asleep under satin and lace spreads. If her mother found she had to wait to be served, she came out to say, 'Come in with me,' but Minna always said, 'I don't feel like it,' and stayed outside with the dogs leashed to the fire hydrant or near the grates protecting the spindly trees.

This Saturday her mother went to Ederle's for the weekend meat. Minna felt like going into the butcher store now and then. She enjoyed sliding her feet slowly in the sawdust, she liked watching Mr. Ederle scrape the bloody innards of chickens from his convex block into a barrel. She liked his straw hat and bloodstained apron, and the piece of liverwurst he cut from the fat roll and gave her on occasion. 'It tasted of flesh and blood,' she thought, 'it was soft and spiced her mouth, it was loving on her tongue and teeth. It needed no chewing to be swallowed.'

Mr. Ederle's older brother, the Other Mr. Ederle, sat inert, wearing his white coat and straw hat in his glass cage. 'He is partly paralyzed,' her mother once explained to her in a whisper, 'and can no longer cut meat.' Minna watched him reach out with his stiff left hand to sweep the change and the dollar bills toward him and into a box on his lap. He could not smile or speak. Once his hat had fallen down to his nose, so that his eyes disappeared from view. This drumble of a man Minna thought of as part of herself; he entered into her being. While she waited for her mother to inspect Mr. Ederle's offerings, make her choice and leave her order, Minna stood rigidly, emulating a paralyzed person, her eyes fixed on the motionless man, finding out in this way what it was like to be the Other Mr. Ederle.

The butcher Mr. Ederle said, 'That all for today, Mrs. Grant?'   'That's all, thank you. Send it.'   'Alvayss. Alvayss,' said Mr. Ederle in his thick German accent. 'Ve alvayss deliver.' Minna broke her trance and took her mother's hand. When they were back in the dappled sun of Amsterdam Avenue she said, remembering the beheaded chickens, 'I know something everyone is afraid of.'   'What, dear?'   'The dark.'   Her mother said, 'I was, when I was little.'   'Are you now?'   Her mother hesitated. Then she said, 'Sometimes I am.'

In front of Gristede's grocery store they met a stout lady in a rumpled white dress cinched in tight at her waist. She wore a decorated khaki soldier's cap. 'Buy a poppy? Made by veterans.' When her mother stopped, the lady said, 'I sell them for the American Legion Auxiliary, *not* for myself,' as though she were accusing Minna and her mother of misunderstanding her motives. Her mother took a nickel from her coin purse and put it into the slot in the lady's tin can. The American Legion lady twisted the green stem of a red poppy to Minna's jumper strap and turned away to stop another person. 'Who is she?'   'She sells poppies to make us remember the men who died in the war.'   'Did you know those men?'   Her mother paused for a long time and then said, 'I don't think I did.' She moved her stern lips so that they appeared to Minna to be crooked with sadness.

Gristede's grocery man took down the things her mother had on her list and put them into a box. A few he could not reach on the top shelves. To Minna's pleasure he removed these with a long stick topped with what looked to be thin steel fingers. They curled around the can of Babo and the box of Corn Flakes and then opened obediently to drop the object into the Gristede man's hand. 'Deliver?' he always asked, although Minna knew this was foolish. Her mother never carried home the meat or groceries. 'Yes, please,' her mother told him. 'Before twelve.'

They walked on toward the bakery. Her mother's comforting warmth turned harsh when they were on the streets. 'Don't step on those places,' her mother warned her. She pulled her violently away from the double-doored metal plates level with the sidewalk cement. Every store had them;

it was the way the storekeepers got to the basement spaces under their businesses. An almost invisible handle lifted the doors and raised them up to reveal metal stairs that went down to the dark, smelly pit of the cellar floor. The cavity was often filled with terrible, odorous water that had collected there since the last rain. Minna's mother was certain that sometimes the doors reversed themselves and dropped down, catapulting the unwary walker to the black hole beneath. 'Stand back. Stay away. Jump over. Come here,' her mother called to Minna if she strayed from the safe pavement to the threatening space. 'Will I drown if I fall in?' Minna asked, panicked by the fear in her mother's voice. Minna had never seen the metal doors turn inside, but she was willing to believe, with her mother, that the old city of New York was full of menace, in need of repair, on the point of swallowing careless inhabitants into the bowels of its infernal underground.

Minna's mother, Hortense, was ridden by other great fears. When she was a child in Mallow, County Cork, two of her older brothers and a young sister had died of what she called 'the white plague.' If Minna was found to have lost half a pound during her semiannual visit to the doctor, her mother was sure the high color on Minna's fair cheeks and her childishly thin arms and legs were indicative of the tubercular taint. When no night sweats or gory cough developed in her daughter, she abandoned her belief that she had brought the phthisic pestilence from the old country (which she had left at sixteen, a hostage to a Jewish-American family who brought her over to be a maid in their household). Instead she centered on a greater dread: polio. She made Minna lie down every afternoon to ensure that she would not become overtired. No tearful 'I don't feel like it' availed. During the heat of the summer, Minna was put to bed, even at the age of ten, with the shade of her room pulled down and left with the stern injunction that she shut her eyes and rest. She tried hard to obey, for by now the fear of polio was almost as strong in her as in her perturbed mother. Minna rehearsed the stories she had been told to make herself more submissive in that hour: about the girl at the summer camp in the Catskills who had been brought home in an ambulance. About the boy who lived in an iron lung that pumped his chest so that he could breathe. About the brothers who lived upstairs in the Grants' apartment house and had been removed to Florida by a frantic mother at the first sign of a head cold. Hortense never ran short of such tales. Always there was a new one to preface each hour of required rest. Minna lay there, longing to read the book she had just brought home from the public library but afraid that the very act of opening its cover might precipitate a crooked leg, a ruined arm.

Minna preferred Central Park to any other place on earth, and in particular, the infinite potentialities of The Rocks. 'Let's please go to The Rocks,' she begged her *Fräulein* when she was very young. Later she coaxed her mother past Columbus Avenue and across Central Park West and into the park at Eighty-sixth Street, where The Rocks loomed up on the right side of the path, grandly striated, elevated here, flattened out there. Out of these rocks Minna created all manner of natural and architectural wonders. Creeping up their sides in her sneakers, she imagined she had reached the peak of an alp, or the tower that imprisoned the English princes, even the Palisades, which, from her safe side of the Hudson River, filled her with awe.

Sometimes other children joined her on The Rocks. Together they would devise games involving storming the accommodating rocks become ramparts or stockades or the Bastille. But Minna much preferred to have The Rocks to herself, to populate their gray surfaces with her own soldiers, wild animals, Druids and Vikings. Once, when she was nine, she had an encounter there with a tatty, ragged, painfully thin gray squirrel. Seated at the top of the highest Himalaya and surveying her base camps, she watched him arrive on the ledge below her. He squatted, turned slightly away from her so that his ugly rodent's profile was toward her. One malevolent eye was fixed upon the first little girl to conquer Mount Everest. He wrapped his paws around his scrawny stomach and cocked his long, slanted head so that now both his evil-looking eyes watched her. Through the transparent skin of his mean ears she could see sunlight that turned them red and sore-looking.

To Minna, the squirrel seemed to be in a state of un-containable fury. His meager tail, like a banner, furled along his haunches, then rose abruptly at the end and appeared to be jerking in convulsions. Stock-still, he was clearly challenging her territorial rights. Was he planning to make the ascent and plant his tail on her peak?

She sat without moving, unrelenting, staring into his eyes. A breeze from the Reservoir moved the fur on his back. Then his frosted tail shook hard in a new spasm of anger. '*Ka-ka-ka,*' the squirrel said, as if his teeth were chattering. With every syllable, his tail trembled. Minna considered answering. Instead she said, 'Scat,' and ham-mered her feet on The Rocks.

The squirrel remained motionless, undaunted by the sounds of thunder over his head. Minna was now very frightened. She believed he was about to assault her position, like the roving Indians on the Mesa Verde. If he came closer she planned to retreat, surrender, ease herself off the cliff and down the other side. When he did move, after the long quiescent session during which both sides seemed on the brink of a truce or exhaustion, Minna, lulled by the impasse, was not prepared. The squirrel made an arced leap, his ears blazing, his far-apart eyes seeming to have coalesced at the front of his head, his tail aloft like a spinnaker at the rear of his flattened back. He landed on her bare, outstretched leg. Minna screamed at him and brought her knees up to shake him off, but not before he had bitten her knee with his small pointed teeth. Then he flipped backward, ran to cover in the bushes across the pathway and disappeared over the culvert and into the Eighty-sixth Street transverse.

The emergency room. Her mother crying beyond the swinging doors. The doctor holding the needle up to the light, filling its tube with white liquid by pushing with his thumb. The ugly swelling. The hurt. Shot after shot. Nausea. Her mother at her bedside in the dark of early morning to feel her forehead. Worst of all, in her mind's eye, the conquering squirrel squatting in his lair under the transverse, gloating over her defeat, measuring the swelling on her knee with his single detached eye and judging it a more than adequate victory. There he sat, triumphant beast who had usurped her throne, in command of all his wicked eyes could survey, challenging her now to ascend the gray cliffs and meet him in mortal combat. Her mother's hydrophobic terror as well as the memory of the terrible shots stayed with Minna all her life. She never returned to The Rocks, the scene of her ignominious defeat, the loss of her own, true place to the mad, victorious mammal.

Before the service elevator was installed in their apartment house, each kitchen was equipped with a manual means of bringing up their groceries. The delivery boy placed his box into the dumbwaiter and pulled the ropes at its sides, raising it to the second level. Then the boy, usually an elderly Irishman who had worked for Gristede's for most of his life, would walk up the stairs, ring the back-door bell and inform the lady of the house or the maid that the groceries were coming up.

Minna loved to be present when the dumbwaiter doors were opened. She would watch the box of food removed by the maid and think of something appropriate to send back down. Once, near Christmas, she took two shirts from her father's pile of starched and laundered white shirts, thinking that the gray-headed delivery boy could well benefit from her well-to-do Jewish father's abundance. Another time she sent down the remains of a lunch she did not like, still on the Limoges plate on which it had been served to her and covered with a damask napkin, on the theory that Mr. Sudermann, the superintendent, might enjoy her despised tuna fish and rice, her mother's usual choice for Friday fare.

At Easter of her seventh year she packed her two-year-old Christmas doll into an oversize Dobbs hatbox from her mother's closet and sent her down on the dumbwaiter to the lower depths from which, Minna hoped, she would never reappear. Mr. Sudermann brought her back promptly. That was the beginning of many such descents on the part of the hated and feared doll. Once she returned seated atop the washed sheets the laundress had sent up from the basement tubs. Seeing the Christmas doll again, risen from the cellar, made Minna believe that nothing could escape the inevitable order of her mother's household. She was convinced that all servants, delivery boys and elevator boys were her mother's agents, and that her Easter faith in the Resurrection was not only a theological belief but a natural, ordinary, everyday event.

> '*Crystal Lake, to you we sing our praises.*
> *Crystal Lake, we'll prove that none can faze us,*'

sang the freshman and sophomore campers. Their faces were lit by the dying campfire, their open mouths looked hollow and black, their eyes glowed with pleasure. Only Minna, recovering from a case of the runs, as her counselor, Fritzie, called it, or the trots, as her bunkmates said, looked glum and felt gloomy. She thought the camp songs were silly. Next to Central Park, the woods of the Catskills looked like a jungle. She was certain that killer insects, vicious chameleons, wild cats and poisonous snakes lurked just beyond where she was sitting. She was worried about the walk back to the bungalows through the dark tangle of trees that grew between the lakeshore where the campfires were held, and the clearing where they all slept: 'Anything could be in there,' she thought. She was afraid of trees in the dark. To her their shapes seemed human, their branches like arms, their leaves like hair. She thought of the lights along Eighty-sixth Street, of the birthday lunch she and her mother would have had at Schrafft's on Broadway if her parents had not insisted she go to camp in July, 'for the experience,' her father had said. She had hated spending yesterday, her eighth birthday, among strangers, having to go to the bathroom all the time. The camp directors had been told, she guessed, so the camp sang the sappy happy birthday song to her at breakfast and presented her with a white cake (she hated white icing) after dinner. Even her counselor, pretty, plump Fritzie, had been a perfect stranger to her until two weeks ago. She liked Fritzie all right, especially at night, when she seemed to sympathize with Minna's fears and took her hand walking away from the rec hall movie to go back to the freshman bunk.

> 'There is a camp for girls
> Close to my heart,'

sang the whole camp. Minna's heart pounded. The girl next to her reached out. Minna said, 'I don't feel like it,' and sat stolidly while all the others held hands. She recognized the song as the usual last one of the night, and decided to go in search of Fritzie to make the first claim on her hand.

She found her at the other end of the large circle, seated far back from it under a tree with another counselor, a very pale, thin person they called Flynn—a name Minna thought strange for a girl—who taught arts and crafts. As Minna came closer she could hear the two counselors having some kind of an argument. She heard Fritzie's high, sweet voice say, 'No! No!' She sounded angry but Minna could not make out what Flynn said. She saw Flynn put an arm around Fritzie's shoulders and bend her head forward toward Fritzie. Suddenly Fritzie stood up and pushed Flynn away, making her lose her balance and fall over. Minna caught up to Fritzie as she was walking to the circle, almost falling over the legs of two other campers who also were not holding hands in the circle. 'Can I walk with you? I have to go to the bathroom,' she said. Fritzie looked unhappy, as though she had not liked the campfire either. But she took Minna's hand and said, 'Okay. Come on, let's get moving.'   'Don't you like Flynn?' Minna asked as they walked in advance of the big clumps of campers who were coming away from the fire.   'I like her,' said Fritzie, 'all right.'   'Were you having a fight?'   'No, not a real fight. It was nothing. Forget about it. What were you doing away from the campfire anyway?'   'I didn't feel like singing and holding hands.'   Fritzie laughed. 'That was my trouble too.'   'Are you afraid of the dark? Like me?' Minna asked.   'No,' said Fritzie. Minna was puzzled by her counselor's replies and even more puzzled when, a few days later, the arts and crafts hours were canceled and the freshmen had to have an extra period of field hockey. Minna hated that sport, with all its fruitless running. If you were a left wing as she was always made to be, it was hard to stay parallel with the ball. She told Fritzie she didn't feel like playing field hockey, she was no good at it because people yelled at her to keep running when she was tired and she wanted to have arts and crafts to finish the snakeskin purse she was making for her mother. Fritzie said, 'Okay, stay on your bunk and write your letter. This is Wednesday and you need a letter home to get into the mess hall at lunchtime.' Minna stayed behind, for the first time in sole possession of the bungalow. She was there when Flynn came in carrying a suitcase, said hello to her and went into Fritzie's little room off the campers' bunks carrying a letter. She came out, picked up her suitcase, said good-bye and went off down the line of bungalows toward the camp entrance. Minna went into Fritzie's room and found the letter Flynn had left on Fritzie's pillow, but it was sealed, so she couldn't read it.

She went back and sat on her bunk and, without any warning to herself, burst into tears. Only after her tears had worn out and she had begun to block print: DEAR MOTHER AND DAD, did she realize what was wrong with her. She was homesick for them, for the dark familiar corners of their apartment and her room on the courtyard, for the park, the gray, friendly cement streets, even for the Saturday marketing.

Minna's mother often said, 'I'm going to bed with a book.' From her example Minna learned the pleasures of reading. In her eleventh year the librarian on the ground floor of the St. Agnes branch of the New York Public Library discovered that Minna had read all the books in the children's section. She sent her upstairs with a card that showed she was to be admitted to the adult library, the first significant elevation of her life and the one she was to remember with the greatest sense of accomplishment. But the prospect of all those books appalled her. How did you choose a book? How did you know one book without pictures from another? How could you be sure you would like the one you chose after you had carried it home and settled down in bed with it? She decided on a simple expedient. She took the first book from the fiction shelf, under A, read it that afternoon and evening and returned it the next day on her way home from school. It was almost a year before she realized that the organized logic of the library did not require such rigorous procedures on her part. A sense of vast freedom flooded her. An infinite world of literary possibility and choice opened up before her when she discovered that the laws of one's pleasure were not based upon alphabetical order.

Minna was graduated from the eighth grade of PS 9 in the late spring of her twelfth year. Her career there had been undistinguished. She was bored by readers and textbooks and went on her eccentric way borrowing library books. One teacher, Miss Mulligan, was to remember her with some pride, for she managed to transfer to the attentive Grant girl her own scrupulosity about English grammar. The other teachers thought her a pretty, pleasant and agreeable girl. None of them realized that under her goodness was a large, complex design of fears, transmitted to her by her mother, fears so paralyzing that to her teachers and friends they appeared as admirable manners and model behavior.

At the graduation ceremony Minna was awarded the prize for character. It was regarded as the plum by her classmates. Scholarship was given a medal, but character was rewarded with the munificent sum of twenty-five dollars. 'Now I can have a bicycle,' Minna told her parents.

Hortense Grant was opposed to this plan, had been against it ever since Minna first asked for one for Christmas two years before. She had visions of her daughter crushed beneath the wheels of a truck or thrown to the ground and run over by a taxicab. Leon Grant did not argue with his wife. He had never been able to surmount her tower of fears, phobias and predictions of catastrophes, and long ago had given up trying.

But if her father would not intercede, Minna was determined to win out nonetheless. To her the possession of a bicycle meant freedom to move, a set of wheels to be used to get to the park and even, the longer and more perilous journey to the Drive. Her courage to oppose her mother was enhanced by the award itself. Did she not, after all, have character? She would have been hard put to define that sonorous word. To her it signified resistance to authority or at least a firm, unwavering stand on matters important to her. Possession of a bicycle, for example.

She would trust no one to hold her prize check until her father brought home the cash for it from his haberdashery store on the Bowery. Minna said, 'Tomorrow is the day I go for my bike.' Her father smiled. 'Remember, you keep it in the basement and walk it on the sidewalk to the park. Eighty-sixth Street is too busy to ride on.' Her mother, who seemed to have surrendered wordlessly to the fated purchase, said nothing more.

To Minna the new bicycle was the most beautiful object in the world. Its fenders were painted white, the metal tubes of the framework were red, the handlebars cuffed in ridged black rubber, comfortable and reassuring to the hand. When she reversed the pedals the brakes instantly responded, like magic. The wheel spokes shone and flashed as they turned, and the saddlelike seat, which could be raised or lowered, felt strong and supportive when she rode. Dolly Sudermann also had a bike, an elderly remnant of her father's Oslo boyhood. The two girls kept their bicycles together in the washroom in the basement, near the dumbwaiter.

In the early days of June, when New York throws off its old age of winter and becomes, in the bright sun and clear air, young and new again, and before summer camp in the

Catskills was imposed upon the reluctant Minna, the two girls met every day in the basement and helped each other bring their bicycles up the steps. On the day of the great neighborhood excitement, they started to walk to the park, their bikes pushed along at their sides. They were discussing their favorite subject, their beloved machines. Dolly's was sturdier and had a more interesting history. Minna's, they agreed, was fancier and technologically more advanced. At the corner of Columbus Avenue they saw a little clutch of police cars. 'An accident,' said Dolly. They could see no broken glass in the gutter, no remains of tires or cars with battered fenders. A crowd had gathered on the sidewalk in a thick circle. The girls came closer but were unable to enter the circle to see what everyone was looking at. A policeman called, 'Stand back. Stand back.' They heard then the high whine of an approaching ambulance. The crowd, almost as one, turned toward the gutter, where, in a moment, an ambulance backed between the police cars. Two men carrying a stretcher leaped out of the rear of the ambulance. The girls put the stands down over the rear wheels of their bicycles and followed the attendants into the midst of the crowd.

'Mr. Weisfeld,' said Dolly. Minna recognized the old man who ran the cigar store on the corner, a pie-shaped little place where her father bought Camels and newspapers and where she and Dolly purchased penny candy to sustain them on their way to the park every afternoon. Mr. Weisfeld lay on his back, his eyes fixed on the sky as if he were searching for birds and planes. The gray sidewalk under his head was now stained red, so red that the blood looked false, like the tomato sauce Minna had seen a character shed in a stage play. 'Is he dead?' whispered Minna.   'I can't tell,' Dolly said. 'He looks dead.'

Minna's heart beat so loud and fast that she found it difficult to breathe. She gulped and lowered her head to stare instead at her brown oxfords. 'O God, make him alive,' she said to herself. She prayed for Mr. Weisfeld because he was an old man and very nice to them always with his licorice and Maryjanes and did not deserve to die this way, stretched out on the dirty cement full of blackened gum pieces and dog stuff, his blood coloring the cracks in the cement.

'Who shot him?' she whispered to a man beside her wearing a yarmulke. 'I don't know. Someone said he wouldn't pay protection. The mob, someone like that.' 'What does that mean, protection?' she asked Dolly, but Dolly whispered, 'I don't know.' The man in the yarmulke had moved away toward the outer rim of the circle. White-coated attendants lifted Mr. Weisfeld onto the stretcher, taking great care, as if he were alive, so Minna took heart. They raised him from the sidewalk and walked with short steps to the ambulance. The policemen were pushing everyone away. 'Disperse,' said one of them to Minna and Dolly. At once, obediently, they started toward their bicycles. As Minna turned away she saw it: what remained on the gray sidewalk of Mr. Weisfeld, a curved, almost transparent piece of skull, like an eggshell, thin and red-tinted, lying where his head had been. A few gray hairs protruded from it. 'O God, did you see that?' Minna asked Dolly. 'What?' 'That—that piece of Mr. Weisfeld they left there?' 'No, I didn't. Where?'

But Minna had seen it, and would see it many times in black dreams, in her morose fantasies, for the rest of her life. Her vision had fallen upon the residue of a life she had known briefly and a death she had almost witnessed, a minute piece of a person left behind to meld into the anonymous walk.

Oh yes, the bicycle. A month to the day after Minna spent her character money on her heart's desire, the bicycle was stolen from the basement and never recovered. Mr.

Sudermann suspected one of the delivery boys, who had been dazzled by the newness and beauty of the machine. Dolly's bike beside it remained untouched. But it could not be proven—the bicycle was gone forever. Hortense sympathized with Minna; inwardly she rejoiced. Leon, who controlled the family purse strings, doling out allowances to both Hortense and Minna, made no offer to replace it. Minna wept and was angry after her mother suggested that the loss may well have saved her life. But when her sadness passed, Minna, accustomed to small shocks to her bland and protected existence, became philosophical and accepted her loss as a fitting test. Still, the price was high, and she resolved never to have character, whatever that meant, again.

For those who were adolescents in the early thirties the high tor of drama was the kidnapping of the Lindbergh baby. For Minna it was her first taste of suspense. She was to weigh other great events always against the state of heightened emotion and tension in which she lived for the seventy-two days of the search. Gabriel Heatter, a radio commentator, called the missing child Little Lindy. When he spoke these words, his voice rang with unctuous sympathy. Over and over, night after night at the supper hour, Heatter rehearsed the heartrending details of the taking of the child from the famous family's house in New Jersey. The whole nation hung upon each subsequent development. Minna never missed his reports, so that Heatter's voice, rolling and damp with anxiety, became the vehicle of her memory. From it she learned the names of the places: Sourland for the Lindbergh estate, and Hopewell, the nearest town. They fell into a Dickensian pattern of significant meaning for her remembered version of the story. Minna thought the names were bestowed on the shocking drama by a higher power with literary pretensions. The whole maternal population of the country, especially in the cities close to the affected area, was filled with apprehension. Mothers accompanied their young children to school and waited for them outside the buildings at three o'clock, under the conviction that kidnapping, like cholera and diphtheria, was catching and would now reach epidemic proportions to threaten their own offspring. Students and teachers at Minna's high school took the cause of the lost baby to themselves. Everyone prayed in assembly for his safety. Newspapers sold out every edition whether they had anything to add to the saga or not, while the *Daily News* and the *Mirror* made certain that black headlines of small import covered their front pages daily. Sales of radios rose dramatically all over the country.

When a small body was found barely two miles from the Lindbergh compound and identified by Little Lindy's weary father (still referred to as Lucky Lindy in the news reports), the story reached every home, every business place and the streets in a matter of minutes. Theater managers interrupted motion-picture performances to inform the patrons, just as the Pathé News was about to start. At Hunter College High School, Minna and her friends heard the grisly news from their history teacher, who had turned on the radio in the teachers' room during the lunch hour. The girls cried, holding one another's hands. Afterward they vowed retribution upon the kidnappers if they should be caught. Nothing would be too awful for punishment, they all decided, wiping their tears and grimly determining the nature of the torture to be inflicted. Outside, many of the city's church bells rang out in a constant tintinnabulation, the rectors, priests and rabbis of the city's religious institutions having decided in advance that God and His vengeful legions should not be left out of current events.

The drama went on and on. Minna stopped reading her daily book and sat close to the Stromberg-Carlson every evening while the search for the kidnappers continued. When a rough-looking carpenter who was unfortunate enough to be German passed along one of the ransom bills, Hortense sighed with relief. Her daughter, her sole concern, was safe, and the guilty Hun, as the tabloid newspapers referred to him, was surely to be executed almost at once. The trial, to everyone's way of thinking, was a mere formality. Minna hung on every word communicated to her by Gabriel Heatter, about the evidence, the cross-examinations, the unlikely story told by the guilty man, the incriminating ladder, the family's unassuaged grief. She held her breath until the conviction was announced, and in unison with her friends expressed the fervent belief that execution in the electric chair should take place immediately.

On the day of the execution, Minna was home from college for spring recess. Hortense and Leon ate their dinner while the radio was playing, eager to know all the details of the monster's death. By dessert they had heard it all. But Minna could eat nothing after Heatter told of the attached wires and the moment of the three jolts that ran through the body of the convicted man, burning the skin of his hands and feet, avenging in a few seconds the vicious murder of a child who had not been permitted to live until its second birthday. Leon Grant left the table, announcing he was going back downtown to work, Hortense took Minna in her arms and held her tight for a minute. Then they went to their rooms, as if the event just concluded required some kind of sacramental separation.

Minna lay on her bed, looking out of the window at which the first great terror of her life had appeared, thinking of the Christmas doll still wrapped up on the floor of her closet, and the remains of Little Lindy decayed beyond recognition but safely laid in the family plot. The whole frightful drama was over. Minna resisted going back to her bland existence, to the everyday world of collegiate good behavior and obedient citizenship. What would now provide color and tension in her life? She realized that she had been living for four years in a great piece of national theater, experiencing a heightened sense of what the spectacle of death could provide to the ordinary private life. She was disappointed that it was over, reluctant to return to the letdown realities of Hortense's smothering love, Leon's cheerful businessman's dishonesties and the dull rituals of college. Now for the first time, she understood the power of an historic event, which surely what they heard about the Lindbergh case was, and the growing importance it had to her life.

At thirteen Minna developed a stammer. An elocution teacher to whom the English teacher sent her said it was nerves. She added that girls almost never stammered, which made Minna's affliction even more mysterious. 'I try . . . n-n-not to,' she said, but effort made it worse. The harder she struggled the more difficult it was to talk. When she volunteered to answer a question in class, her attempts produced visible grimaces of annoyance on the faces of her classmates, and terrible embarrassment for Minna. Finally, Michael Casey, the principal, intervened. Hortense was asked to visit the school. 'She is not doing well in academic subjects, and her speech is, well . . . very bad,' Michael Casey told Mrs. Grant. Hortense found this impossible to believe. She knew about the stammer, to a small extent, but since Minna had grown quite silent in her adolescence, it had not seemed important to her. But academic subjects! Hortense believed Minna was close to being a genius, a wonderfully endowed, intellectual girl. Principal Casey went on, 'The home arts department here is very good.' Mrs. Grant would hear no more. With only five years of formal schooling herself (before her tenant-farmer father shipped her, his first of ten children, to America), Hortense had an inordinate respect for academic subjects. She argued with the principal and at last was able to persuade him to retest Minna with the new Binet-Otis test she had read about, designed to establish her intelligence quotient. In this way Minna convinced him she could be readmitted into Civics, World History, and Regents English. Saved from tutelage in the arts of cooking and sewing, Minna knew she had to settle her attention on academics, as Principal Casey referred to the subjects she had been neglecting.

One of the reasons for her failures in the past was clear: Minna had developed a passion for swimming. Her high school did not have a pool, but after school there was one within walking distance, in a Salvation Army building. There, every afternoon, the club to which she belonged met. They named themselves the Gertrude Ederle Swim Club eight years after their idol became the first woman to swim the English Channel. The club worshipped the conqueror of those brutal waters; they had memorized every detail of her life and great effort. Hortense had been nervous about swimming, for she feared water and had spent her entire passage to America under the covers in her bunk in the room on the *Mauritania* she shared with three other girls going to be maids in New York households. But Hortense saw Minna swim in a meet in the last days of summer camp. She allowed her to join the club, believing there was safety in numbers: twelve girls trained together every afternoon and long hours on the weekend, practicing their Australian crawl, their resting tread, their flips and turns. Their ambition was to swim the Channel.

Minna's relationship to water was loving. Moving in it, she felt alive, clean, respected and clever. Her body had developed and was now slender and well shaped, although she was not very tall. Her shoulders broadening with the crawl, her hips remained narrow under the exercise of her rhythmic kicking. Her body was suited to movement in the element she found preferable to any other. Looking at her friend and swimming partner, Emma Lifson, by far the best swimmer among the dozen, Minna enjoyed the changes that came about in her own person since she had fallen in love with the water. Emma was a solid, husky, thickset girl, like Minna a single piece of well-integrated machinery but a log to Minna's twig.

Minna was exhilarated by the perfect, mindless movements of her arms and legs. Her small, blond, handsome head (she had to concede her own good looks, looking at Emma in the dressing room) stretched in a straight line with her body as she pulled along the surface of the water, making a smooth, thoughtful progress without once breaking her stroke, always thinking about Gertrude Ederle. (From Cape Griz-Nez to Dover on August sixth, nineteen hundred and twenty-six, in fourteen hours and thirty-one minutes, through choppy two-foot waves, the waters of the Channel inhospitable to the twenty-year-old swimmer.) She turned by flipping over neatly, pushing away from the green side of the pool and pressing on with her inexorable Australian crawl. (The daughter of a German butcher with a store on Amsterdam Avenue, a member of the Women's Swimming Association at thirteen, an Olympic gold medal hung on her broad chest at eighteen for her heroic part in the free-style relay team's efforts, tangled with two bronze medals for the one hundred meter and the four hundred meter races.) Minna rehearsed all the details as she swam, trusting example to spur her on. Stroking hard, she pictured seven black-framed certificates hanging in the Ederle family house in Queens awarded for Gertrude's amateur triumphs, one for each of her world records before she was nineteen.

Minna swam beside Emma Lifson. Stroke for stroke they matched each other, pushing for five miles. Minna pounded relentlessly against the low-choppy pool water. (Against the cutting sea for almost thirty interminable miles, close to the boat operated by her trainer Thomas Burgess, near and yet far enough away from it not to be tempted by the prospect of relief by holding, even briefly, to the side for warm tea in her frozen esophagus, for soup she knew he carried with him in the hold, unable to hear anything because the slashing sea slammed against her ears, she was almost blinded by the wall of water every time she turned her head and raised it to breathe.)

All Minna's resources were required for her to finish her prescribed miles. From some hidden spring she brought up Gertrude's example, re-creating her unsuccessful first swim, when the appalling sea had conquered Gertrude two miles from the harbor of Dover. Her frozen mouth gasping for air, instead had sucked in saltwater. She gagged and threw up into the spume that crashed over her head. Minna felt herself sinking with Gertrude when Thomas Burgess reached out to grab her. Even then Gertrude tried to shake herself free of his rescuing hands. 'Come out,' Burgess said. She spit water at his hand and said, 'What for?' But at last she had to surrender to the rejection of the hostile sea.

Pushing the water against its will, it seemed to Minna, she reached and kicked to travel the last laps. (Twelve months later Ederle had returned to the same malignant waters, her spirits bolstered by small sums of money given her by the *Daily News* and the *Chicago Tribune*, to whom she promised 'the jump' over the other papers for her personal story when she made it. In the boat this time was a famous journalist named Westbrook Pegler, accompanied by his wife. He was there as a ghost, the man the *Chicago Tribune* had hired to put words to her every stroke, her every hard breath, to the moment that she felt the bottom under her at Dover and changed from fish to woman, erect and triumphant.)

Minna and Emma Lifson finish their stint in the pool at almost the same moment as Minna sees Gertrude step ashore, rejecting Thomas's offered support, weary but still strong. 'What now?' Gertrude is wondering. She falls heavily upon the pier, scraping her thigh, and sees her body is black with the Channel's fishy wastes. A man in a blue uniform (yes, this is history) steps up to her as she lies gasping on the dock, and bends down. 'May I see your passport?' he says.   'What else?' she says to herself.

While Minna dresses she turns her reverie to talk and tells Emma about Gertrude Ederle. She will visit her German forebears in the Black Forest for a few weeks, see the village that bred her extraordinary physique. Bushels of wastepaper and ticker tape will rain down on her as she rides up Broadway in an open car between Mayor Jimmy Walker and Grover Whalen, the official greeter for celebrities. For this great occasion she wears her cloche hat over her close-cropped hair, her straight black tie holding together the starched collar of her man's shirt, her suit jacket buttoned stiffly over the rugged chest and arms that had subdued the Channel. She will spend eight weeks in the company of Hollywood stars making a foolish movie called *Swim Girls Swim*, in which she will appear as the instructor of champion Gertrude Ederle, played by the beautiful and curvaceous Bebe Daniels. She will sign her name to a paragraph endorsing the virtues of an insect destroyer call Flit. Holding the long metal tube in one hand, the plunger in the other, dressed in her familiar tank suit and still wearing her Channel-conquering white cap, she stands at the edge of a Hollywood pool, ready to assault hordes of large pests, looking strapping, muscular, flat-footed, thick-hipped, the very model of courage and stoutheartedness.

'What is it with you and Gertrude Ederle?' Emma asked.   'I don't know. I guess I like great swimmers, and success stories. And my mother's afraid of the water,' said Minna and laughed.

Minna was first to drop out of the Gertrude Ederle club. She felt the pressure of approaching graduation. Preparing to take the entrance examination for Barnard College, she had to read the books on the Regents' required list she had blithely ignored for so long. After two years of illusory aquatic freedom, she returned to the dry ground of *Silas Marner*, *Ethan Frome* and *The Old Curiosity Shop*, to memorize the organization of the government of the State of New York, and to acquire (with a tutor her parents provided for her) some dim idea of what biology and trigonometry were about.

Unfortunately, it was true. Minna's psyche was now formed, perhaps deformed. She was destined to be an anxious young woman, filled with inherited and communicated maternal fears, and compounded with some she had herself contributed to her affrighted spirit. Even swimming eventually became a source of dread. Once, in a pool footbath, she believed, she caught a lingering case of athlete's foot. After that she swam only in fresh water or, as she said she preferred, in the Atlantic Ocean. She plunged into rough waves, white water, voracious breakers, diving without hesitation, it seemed. And every time, without exception, she was terrified, as though the ocean were an enemy, the sum total of her fears, the culminative phobia that canceled out the fading pleasure of her youth and made itself part of the ferocious and threatening world around her.

THE ODORS OF ONE'S PAST. Maud Mary Noon believed they clung to the inside of the nostrils like snot. It is not true that we do not remember them. Often Maud told Minna and Liz about the cold days of winter in her early childhood in the tiny Hudson River village of New Baltimore. She was made to play outside in the snowy yard after her mother came home from the night shift at the hospital in Albany, seventeen miles north of the village. It was Maud's belief that her mother sang and rocked the sick and dying to sleep in the hospital. This was what she meant by 'having the duty.' 'Duty' was the word used by her mother for her work. 'I have the night duty,' she would say to Maud and her brother, Spencer. Maud considered duty to be warmth and comfort. It meant to reach out with maternal, antiseptic hands, to hold patients in her starched white arms.

Maud's brother was older. In her memory Spencer always seemed to be in the seventh grade in the red-brick grade school up the hill from them. On her mother's duty nights the two children stayed at home by themselves, locking the door after their mother went to catch the bus to Albany. Maud relished the phrase 'catch the bus.' She had a vision of her mother's flat white hand thrust forward into the road to pull the moving bus toward her, like the gold ring on a merry-go-round. 'Gone away to catch the bus, away, away to catch the bus,' she would sing to Spencer during the long evenings they were left together.

Maud was five and liked being left home with Spencer who was *old*, twelve. He was offhand with her but kind, like a preoccupied hunter with his admiring dog. The house was very quiet. From the parlor windows she watched boats on the river, the moving string of lights over black water, tankers mostly, and some small shadowy white yachts and tugs working their way noisily to the port of Albany.

Maud told Spencer the boats were going to their night duty. He listened to her fancies absently, for he was usually intent on his homework or on an old train set he was repairing. It had been given to him by Mr. Rossi, who raised mushrooms in dark sheds in Ravena, the next town to theirs, and had belonged to Rossi's son Angelo, now grown up and become a priest. So intent was Spencer on restoring the caboose that Maud had to make her river-traffic observations over and over again. Finally he would grin at her. He never answered, but she knew he had heard and was satisfied. If he said anything at all to her queer ideas it would be to call her by the pet name he had given her: 'O Beastie!' She never minded it, because she could discern the affection in his voice. She loved Spencer dearly in return, and she knew, even then, that she was indeed an ugly little girl.

Spencer and Maud had adjoining bedrooms. When she was very little, the solid sliding door between their rooms was kept open. But later Spencer began to have secret projects, plans he wrote down on the left-hand blank pages of discarded ledgers from the mushroom plant, notes he didn't want anyone to see, things he was planning to build out of his father's stores of wire and silver paper. Later still, he had other occupations that took him to his bed in late afternoon. Maud could hear the springs of his bed making tinny, tuneless sounds. Once he pulled the door shut, he told her never to try to open it, and she never did. She listened to the sounds behind the door, the dropping of tools, Spencer talking to himself, his contented sighs accompanying the rasps of the bedsprings. From her exclusion she learned valuable lessons: she knew more about the nature of reality when it was hidden from her or merely suggested to her, lessons, her roommate Liz told her, that were well known to photographers.

Maud never minded Spencer's shutting himself away. So great was her fondness for him that she felt protected from behind the door, knowing that he was there. She felt safe going to sleep, and happy when she woke in the morning to hear the thumping, rushing, banging sounds of Spencer dressing for school. Sometimes Maud knelt on her bed and crooked her neck so she could watch him from her window walking up the road from their house to the school she knew was there but had not yet been to. She could see his back covered by the heavy plaid coat with a belt which he wore all the time he was growing up until it became small enough to be made into a jacket. His books swung from his bare hand by a strap and his other hand was always in his pocket, pockets being their mother's suggested substitute for gloves. Their cat, a narrow brindled tomcat named Flo (for their mother, Florence, who in turn had been named, providentially, for Florence Nightingale) would follow him to the top of the hill and then come back to wait for Maud to come out later on. Flo was not allowed in the house, ever. Their mother thought cats stole the breath from babies and made older children sneeze.

The air left behind in the house by Spencer seemed protective, friendly, patient, to Maud. Close to nine o'clock, a little later in the winter when the roads were bad, her mother walked down the hill from where the bus had dropped her off. 'Drop me off here,' Maud once heard her say to a bus driver in Albany. The command became part of her childhood litany. 'Drop me off, drop me off, drop me off at the river,' she sang, standing on their veranda. Maud watched her mother come toward the house, her face a puffy canvas of weariness, the white strip of her uniform showing from the bottom of her coat. She took her fingers out of her mouth to wait for the sound of the key in the door. The house atmosphere felt less cosy once her mother was home. The air grew crisp and taut, strung tight by the knowledge Maud had that she was not part of her mother's duty. In a rush Maud put on her union suit and then tried to press over its stiffened legs the cotton stockings that were still damp and yellow from yesterday. Still wearing her heavy coat and the crocheted hat that covered her ears and tied under her chin, her mother came upstairs. 'Hi there, little Beastie,' she said, and helped her on with her middy blouse and black tie, two sweaters and the leggings that buttoned up the sides of her legs, covering the instep of her shoes. Always her mother asked her if she had washed, and often Maud lied and said, 'Yes, I did.'

They went downstairs together to a breakfast of rolled oats left in the double boiler by Spencer and the remains of the dinner biscuits spread with colorless margarine. Maud tried to swallow some of the icy, almost crystallized milk her mother kept in a cold box on the back porch. She loved to watch her mother undress in the kitchen, standing over the floor outlet to the gas furnace. Florence hung her uniform behind the dining room curtains above her white shoes, putting wooden sticks, like small curved arrows, into them.

'Now I need my sleep,' Florence told Maud as she pulled and pushed her galoshes on for her, locking the metal fasteners all the way up over the leggings and clipping her mittens to her coat sleeves. For years Maud could feel the nasty pinch under her chin of the elastic band on her felt hat. Maud took her sled from the back porch, where Florence waited for her, loaded on it her tin pail and shovel, a set of assorted chipped dishes, burned pots and old baking pans. From the snow piles she made pies and cakes, ice soup and granular alabaster roasts with potatoes. She listened for her mother to snap the door lock behind her, trying hard not to cry; she hated to be put out every morning in this way. Outside, the air turned hostile and inhospitable. She played alone out there, with only the elusive Flo to talk to until Spencer came home for lunch and pounded on the back door to wake their mother.

Often, before he came, Maud wanted to be let in, to show her mother the culinary snow marvels she had concocted, or to go to the bathroom. She grew hungry and wanted some biscuits, even a drink of frosty milk. But there was no way to be let in, she understood that. Upstairs, until noon, her mother slept heavily, her rest after the duty guaranteed by the locked door. Maud stayed on the porch, her snow cuisine finished, pestering Flo when she could catch her, sometimes crying to herself, watching for Spencer's plaid coat. Every day, as rescue from the opened door drew close, she breathed in the spiced fumes of pee that rose up from her woolen underwear. She felt its warmth in the soles of her galoshes, and watched small dollops of it soak into the bare porch boards.

Maud's father, Joseph Noon, was a middle-aged noncommissioned officer in the supply corps of the United States Army. Proudly sewn to his left sleeve were seven slanted gold dashes representing his many years of service. Maud liked the name for this embroidery, 'hash marks.' She made a poem: 'Hash marks on the sleeve/Khaki cloth and yellow weave/Father's time is called a leave.'

Sergeant Noon came home on holidays and one weekend every month. When Maud was older he took his annual leave in September to give his wife time off for her vacation. Most of his pay was committed to his family. But while he was away in Fort Dix, New Jersey, he told his family he led a contented male existence. He refrained from the familiar indulgences of pool and poker because of the money they involved, instead going to twenty-five-cent movies on the post. He watched card games and smoked with a buddy at the noncommissioned officers club: his limit was two beers a night. Maud always had a clear view of her father's life in camp.

He hardly missed his family, it seemed to her. Florence was his second wife, his first having died of influenza. His two sons from his first family were now raised and 'on their own,' as he often said proudly. One was a toolmaker in Detroit, the other a machinist's mate in the navy. It seemed to Maud, as she grew up, that her father had used his short store of domestic affection on his first family. When he was home now he was silent and withdrawn. His time with Florence and the children was spent doing repairs on the house and waiting for his meals to be served. His interest in the repetition involved in a second family was minimal. Sometimes he had trouble remembering Maud's 'fancy' real name, as he called it. He too called her Beastie.

Maud's father was an absentminded man, always, Maud believed, thinking about the place he had just come from or was due to return to, never really entirely at home. He ignored his handsome son Spencer because he failed to show any interest in guns and things military. He patted Maud on the head now and then because, she thought, he felt sorry for his ugly little girl. But even with these gestures he was not entirely there. In later years, when Maud read Paul Valéry in Otto Mile's class at college, she found that Valéry described a blank piece of paper as 'the absence of presence.' That, in retrospect, described her father.

Joseph Noon's content with his fatherhood was so silent, so reserved, that his children took him to be the model of a patient parent. When Florence went to visit her elderly parents in Gloversville or on her yearly vacation alone, Joseph kept house well, picking up after the children, teaching them to make spare, tight beds with squared corners and unwrinkled sides and tops. He fixed efficient, quick, army-type meals. Everything was accomplished, as he said, 'in lickety-spit.' Until she was older and wanted to use the word in a poem about her father she thought it meant cleaned by means of a saliva-coated tongue.

In her childhood she considered her father's withdrawn forbearance an adequate substitute for tempestuous love, an emotion she understood superficially from reading the novels of Warwick Deeping, her mother's favorite author. When Maud had difficulty getting into her tight bed in the still-warm nights of September, her father would allow her to sleep on top, smiling at her feebleness before the rigidly tucked sheets.

To the small Maud the words 'leave' and 'post' were synonymous with 'duty.' They were what her parents did.

They stood for places and actions in the world beyond New Baltimore in which she played no part. Sometimes her father would turn up unexpectedly in his natty uniform saying he had been given a three-day pass. She extracted the word 'pass' from his arrival and stored it among her cherished collection of poetic words. Standing outside the back door before her sixth birthday, before the first grade rescued her from frozen mornings and the snow she had yellowed, she would recite her incantation: 'duty,' 'leave,' 'pass,' 'post,' a litany directed primarily at the scrawny cat Flo. Later, she came to believe those magical syllables initiated her into the vocation of poet. They taught her a respect for the force of fine, tough, short, Anglo-Saxon words. Her mature style was to hang upon them, solid, simple words, building to the last line of the quatrain. There, in a burst of expansive embrasure, a large, bumbling Latin abstraction appeared, contrasting sharply with the spare materials of the first three lines. Hers was a construction starting on cement footings and rising ethereally into a poetic cosmos.

Summers were dull for Spencer and Maud. Their mother spent her free time fall housecleaning in advance. Fixed in Maud's memory was the summer she was seven. Her parents decided to paint the rough-hewn rafters and walls of her room and Spencer's plaster ceiling. It was the hottest summer on record for upstate New York. Many days the temperature reached one hundred degrees. The pump in the side yard refused to work, the cistern became low, revealing to Maud's horror its usually submerged collection of dead weasels, rats, mice and chipmunks. But still Florence drew water from the cistern while they waited for their father to come home on leave to fix the well. Once Spencer rescued a struggling woodchuck from the water and set him loose near his hole.

During the painting and whitewashing of their rooms, Maud and Spencer were sent to swim in the river. 'The only cool place in the whole northeast,' their father said. In those days the Hudson was clear and clean, a fast-moving river, with its own eccentric current, and very cold. Village kids played and swam there on hot summer days, plunging into the river from wooden boards, a frame for the banks that had been installed when New Baltimore was a supplier of ice to New York City.

At fourteen Spencer was a good swimmer. That summer, when they spent so many hours at the river, he taught Maud to swim. It was easy. She was a little tub of a girl who could float almost at once on her stomach. Quickly she acquired a serviceable dog paddle. When she grew tired she sat on the splintered boards and watched Spencer dive in, over and over again, with the town boys, their brown legs flopping wildly into the blue river. Some less skillful boys took great jumps holding their noses, bending their legs like frogs beneath them. While still airborne they screamed defiance at the passing boatmen, who waved to them from their tugs. Maud ignored the other children her age because their splashings frightened her. She paddled happily in the shallow whorls made by the jumping boys and imagined they were creating little pools for her pleasure.

Always she was aware of Spencer, of his lithe body, his long hands and feet still a little out of proportion to his thin trunk and narrow, blond head. She thought him the most beautiful boy in the world, and told her mother her opinion. 'Boys are handsome, girls are beautiful,' her mother told her. But Maud knew she could not be right. For was she not an ugly girl?

While Joseph Noon was still on leave, and halfway through the work on Spencer's room, Spencer got sick. It was a Saturday, Maud was to remember. Maud and Spencer had come back from a long day on the river, Maud holding on as always to his cold hand as they walked up the steep hill, pleased to be allowed to do so. Three times during the long trudge she felt him shudder. At dinner his face flushed and he had no appetite for the Saturday-night lamb stew. Florence sent him to bed and came up later to put an extra blanket over him.

Maud and Spencer called their mother by her first name, at her request, as soon as they were old enough to know what it was. 'Mother' seemed to them a word for all such persons and did not apply to one particular instance, whereas Florence was the word given to their mother alone. Florence went upstairs again early in the evening to see to him. After Maud had gone to bed, she heard Spencer call, 'Mother,' and so she knew he was sick. She heard him call again a few times during the night, each call sounding more urgent, before Florence was roused from her heavy sleep and came to him. The next morning Spencer had a high fever and pain in his arms and legs. When Maud brought him a glass of milk in the afternoon his eyes were red, as if he had been crying. He told her he could not move his neck. The Ravena doctor was away for the weekend, so Florence relied on her nurse's skills, washing him down, as she said, with cool water and feeding him liquids, which he threw up almost at once.

Maud had understood separation before sickness struck Spencer. Her father exemplified it to her, but she had rarely felt pain at his systematic absences. Separation because of Spencer's illness turned into the terrible anguish of constant loneliness and loss. On the third day of his sickness (Maud remembered that day because it was her seventh birthday but there was no one home to celebrate it with her), her father and Florence took Spencer to the emergency room at the Albany Hospital.

The months of separation from him that followed were

like a deep cut on her knee that festered and scabbed over and then opened whenever she bent it. In September she had to go up the hill to school without him. On Sundays she was allowed to accompany her parents to the hospital during visiting hours. While her parents went in, Maud waited in the parking lot, her eyes fixed on the third-floor windows where, Florence had pointed out to her, the polio ward was. There Spencer lay, breathing in and out with the help of a machine.

Maud could not remember when the word became part of her secret chants. Polio. Polio. Rolio-polio, from roly-poly, the descriptive word her father used to describe her. 'Roly-poly polio.' She whispered the words sadly to herself, feeling in this way that she was part of Spencer's sickness, and close to him. At seven she wrote another couplet: 'Spencer sleeps in an iron lung/Why just one? Why just one?' Maud could not remember how she knew that people had two lungs and never understood why the doctors had chosen to apply the machine to only one. As for her poem, she was surprised at how perfect it was, and amazed that she was able to make up a rhyme almost as good as the poem she was made to learn in first grade: 'I think that I shall never see/A poem lovely as a tree.' While she much admired the famous poem she did not understand the sentiment. How could anyone think an old tree (there were many of them in New Baltimore) was as good as a poem?

Staring up at the blank windows of the polio ward, Maud felt her chest contract. She beat her fists against her sides in fury and gritted her teeth. She wept for loneliness and for her beloved brother: 'Why just one?/Why just one?' she repeated again and again, the question addressed to the brick hospital walls and to God.

In the winter of 1925 Spencer was back at home, always in his bed or a chair, the rafters of his room only half whitened. Maud was now afraid of him and cried when Florence made her bring him something. She always hoped he would be in his bed, not propped up in his chair where she could see his useless leg and arm. He had given up reading because his head often ached, and his projects were abandoned after the strength had gone out of his right arm. Maud believed he had given up talking too, or at least he never said anything to her or called Florence. His silence meant to Maud that he was angry at what had happened to him, angry at the abrupt end to his private life in his room with the door shut.

'Can I get you some water?' 'Are you cold?' 'Do you want the blanket?' 'Are you hungry?' 'Do you know tonight is Halloween?' Every sentence Maud directed to him was a question. But he would not answer except to look at her with his beautiful, low-sunken blue eyes, as though her standing there on her two feet was a reproach to him. He was offended, she believed, by her desire and ability to serve him.

Florence did not work that winter. The family lived very carefully on Joseph Noon's monthly army check. Maud was made to wear Spencer's old plaid jacket to school. In it she felt confused. She felt she had lost herself, the ugly, roly-poly little girl with the fancy, dumb name. Her classmates laughed at her name, and at everything about her, the awkward fat way she had to turn over on her hands and knees before she could get up from the floor during exercises, the way the tip of her fat nose whitened when she drank milk. They thought her thick lips very funny and her heavy glasses a kind of vast joke. Once she wondered whether it was possible that, having fit into Spencer's coat so early, she might metamorphose into her beautiful (no, handsome) brother. She imagined all his old grace flowing into her through the torn lining and yellow-and-green squares of his coat. She was afraid to look at the new, sick, withered Spencer. But she took pleasure in using his old jacket. Her mother had offered it to her at about the same time she was allowed to take four books at a time from the school library. The rest of that long winter of Spencer's slow convalescence was lost to her except for one monumental discovery, that writing words and poems in composition books was as good as saying them over and over to herself, and more permanent.

In June, Florence heard about the Children's Seashore Home in Atlantic City, New Jersey, and told Maud and Spencer about it at dinner. Spencer now had a steel brace on his leg and could move slowly and jerkily with two canes. Florence said she was going to take him to Atlantic City for training and exercise as soon as Joseph came home on leave. She showed Spencer pictures of a long, rambling gray building with wooden ramps instead of steps to every door. 'The Atlantic Ocean is just beyond the edge of the picture,' she said, 'and there is a boardwalk running along it where you can be pushed in wicker chairs by darkies.'

Spencer said, 'I won't go.'   'Why not?'   'Because it's for crippled kids and I'm not a cripple. I'm getting better by myself.'

Maud understood that Spencer saw himself as he used to be. That was how she sometimes saw him too. He was afraid he would be reminded of his true state by the other children in the Home. In spite of his protests, Florence took him to Atlantic City. She stayed in a rooming house on Kentucky Avenue while he was bathed and massaged and exercised in the Home. 'He is having therapy,' she wrote to Maud. 'Therapy' was the word for treatment, a new and lovely word to Maud, one she was to use several times in the poem about her college teacher, Otto Mile, in lines like 'Tendered his eye as therapy/To her crippled poems.'

Once while Spencer was being treated, Florence wandered over to the Boardwalk. It was a warm September day and the Boardwalk was clogged with people. Rolling chairs were lined up along the rail facing the sea. In them sat well-dressed elderly couples, their knees covered with bear rugs despite the heat of the day. Florence inched her way through the crowds until she was just behind the chairs. On the sand below she could see a number of young women in bathing dresses and black stockings posing for a photographer. The women held one hand behind their heads, the other seductively on their hips. The photographer's head was lost under the black drape that covered the back of the camera. All Florence could see of him was his bent body, his white-clad legs behind the three poles of the camera stand.

Florence watched for a time. Then she turned to a stick-thin man beside her. He was wearing a bathing suit and a policeman's cap. 'What is happening down there?'   'A pageant. They're getting ready. To crown the most beautiful girl in the country.'

Florence was too timid to ask anything else. She gazed at a small dark-haired girl who was turning slowly in her place, lifting her feet delicately now and then as though the sand were very hot. As the girl came to face her, Florence saw she wore a white satin ribbon diagonally across her chest from her shoulder to her hip. On it was printed MISS TULSA. Miss Tulsa was, Florence later told Maud, the most beautiful person she had ever seen. Maud imagined Florence felt her own flat, gray and almost formless shape expand into her vision of the dark, shapely beauty. That night on the Million Dollar Pier, in a lavish coronation scene, Florence saw Miss Tulsa crowned Miss America.

Spencer came back from the Home dispirited and not visibly improved. Florence claimed his arm and leg were 'more supple.' But, watching him try to walk, Maud agreed with Spencer: his leg was growing stiffer, having lost entirely the shape of its muscles. Weekly, the straps within the steel brace needed to be tightened around his white, broomstick leg. But it was true that his arm seemed to be somewhat better despite his resentful inertia. 'And it would be better still if you would exercise,' Florence said.

Maud understood Spencer's resistance to doing anything to improve his state of health. His fine, useful body had been dealt a terrible blow, his view of himself as helpful older brother and beloved son was destroyed, and he wanted nothing to do with partial restoration, especially not through his own efforts, which he believed were doomed to disappointment. He refused to walk anywhere except around the downstairs of the house. He gave up his room, the books he had so carefully collected, his half-restored Lionel trains, the mock-up of the Globe Theater he had made in junior high school. Florence was told to bring down only his necessary toilet articles and some of his clothes he called his 'things' and leave them in a corner of the dining room, where his bed was now set up. He refused to go outdoors.

A teacher from the Ravena school district came to see him three times a week and scolded him for never doing his homework or the reading she had assigned him. When Maud came home from school he was always in his special steel chair staring at the little water glass of wildflowers she had picked for him the day before. He took a melancholy pleasure in their moribund state. 'You can't pick them fast enough to stop their dying. Even I know that. They're like people. If they're picked by God or fate, they die before they have a chance to live,' he told Maud, who already knew the truth of this. She saw it clearly illustrated in this brother she loved so much that her throat and chest ached for him.

Her weak eyes were now covered with very heavy glasses she called spectacles, having found that word in *David Copperfield*. 'These are my new spectacles,' she told her classmates. 'Am I not a spectacle in my new spectacles?' she would say, having learned that laughing aloud at herself made her bear the laughter of others with better grace. Had she not laughed first? She was grateful to the heavy glasses. Looking at Spencer made her cry, but he could not see it, she believed, and she could blink away the tears. She hated to watch him struggle to the dinner table, gripping his two canes angrily, dragging his leg. With him, she resented the incomprehensible unfairness of the universe.

But her love for him, now a burden in the face of what had happened, did not have to endure her growing up. When Spencer was almost nineteen, and he and Florence had made the September pilgrimage to Atlantic City for the third time, and the therapy was once again of no apparent use, Spencer seemed to take matters into his own hands, or so Maud was always to think. He caught cold, the cold turned to bronchitis and then, so fast that it was hard to believe, into pneumonia. Joseph was home on leave when it happened. He and Florence took Spencer into Albany in the old Ford station wagon. He was admitted into the hospital, and Florence stayed with him at night, sleeping fitfully in the chair in his room. Joseph spent his days there. In four days, they both returned to New Baltimore, without him.

'Dead? How *could* he be dead?' Maud demanded of Florence. She insisted, 'He cannot be. It cannot be. There is no *way* he can be dead.' Florence was too upset to answer. Joseph, in his removed, stoical, reasonable way, tried to comfort her. 'It might be just as well. He hated being the way he was. A cripple.' Maud cried for so many days that her eyes swelled almost shut. The phrases her father chose to allay her grief infuriated her. 'Maybe he's better out of it.' 'What do you mean, *it?*' 'His misery, you know, his life, the way he was, his arm, his leg, the braces and all,' said Joseph softly, half to the stony Florence, half to his irritating daughter, trying not to look at her swollen, red face.

'It cannot be,' Maud said again and again to no one. Spencer was her childhood, her hope for beauty in the world, her faith in her inner self. She carried around with her a photograph of them together, his hand on her head. The white spaces on the picture turned tan. Across the cracked back he had written, 'To Beastie from her loving brother Spencer Noon.' In that snapshot she is standing stolidly at his side, a square child in a cotton dress with a large bow at the back and another white bow in her hair just above the barrette. Her fists are clenched at her sides and she is scowling into the camera, her eyes slits, the tip of her tongue showing at the side of her mouth. Liz, her college roommate, said she resembled one of the mongoloid children she liked to photograph. Spencer looks sleek and handsome. His white collar is open at his slender neck, his smile is easy and warm. In this way Maud remembered her brother, frozen into that graceful stance, his hand forever on her ugly, angry head, his beautiful eyes fixed eternally into the lens of the photographer.

In the year after Spencer died, and before Joseph was in-valided out of the army, Florence chose a scorching day in August to announce her new plan. 'Next month I'm taking my vacation. Aunt Louise will come to look after Maud.'

Joseph did not look surprised. 'Good for you, your fur-lough. How long?' 'About a week, I think.' 'Oh, fine, fine,' said Joseph. 'The mountains are nice. I once went

44

to a place called Roscoe in the Catskills. It was very nice.'

Maud was thirteen. Since Spencer's death she was often lonely, and she hardly knew Aunt Louise. She said, 'All by yourself?' Maud expected her to say, 'I need a rest,' as she always said to her daughter when she had locked her out of the house after her night duty, but she did not. 'Where are you going?' asked Maud.   'To Atlantic City.' There was silence. Joseph was thinking about the next day, when he was scheduled to go back to Fort Dix. Maud wondered if her mother was going to Atlantic City because Spencer had been taken there so often for his 'cure.' In some strange way, perhaps, Maud thought, Florence hoped to encounter his spirit on the expansive Boardwalk.

The announced vacation never came off. Maud remembered it, even better than Florence's subsequent trips to Atlantic City. That year, her mother's fury knew no bounds. Again and again she heard her tell about the malevolent hotel owners in Atlantic City who wanted to discourage the pageant. They said that the women who had been coming to the city were not good types. They cited affairs that developed and subsequent unsavory divorces among attendants at the pageant. 'Not the contestants, of course, but the men who come to see the pageant and are seduced, you know. Good family men who stay at the big hotels. That's what the owners claim. And the contestants—they say some are vile and obscene.' Maud hung on every word, wanting more details but afraid to ask. 'Ridiculous,' said Florence. 'I've been there once and I've never seen anything like that. The girls are beautiful and innocent, every one of them. Not one of them is even married. All good girls.'

Florence's defense to her family of the morality accompanying the Miss America Pageant was to no avail. For five years the hotel men's determined organization won out. The pageant was suspended, the occupants of the rolling wicker chairs traversed the Boardwalk undisturbed by the sight of girls on the sand revealing their charms in their swimsuits, and Florence took no vacation.

In August 1933 Florence said, 'There's going to be the pageant this year. I'm going.' From then on, she went every year, religiously, as if she were a mendicant on pilgrimage. Each year her life formed a determined parabola. The height of the curve was reached in the early fall with her visit to Atlantic City; the decline occurred after her vacation, when she knew she had eleven months to wait until her return. She became a passionate scholar of the event, avid for all its statistics, much like the lover of sports. She was interested in the given names of the contestants and often regretted not having bestowed one of the more popular ones (Mary, Patricia, Barbara, Carole) upon her daughter. She admired Fay, Lois, Rose, names that more than once had graced the winners. Maud later suspected Florence thought she might have prevented the unfortunate development of her little girl's anatomy if she had bestowed upon her a more auspicious name.

In the winter, Florence's talk was full of such matters as the unusual height of the tallest Miss America, who was five feet eight. Florence herself preferred the smallest winner, five feet one, 'before my time, so I never actually saw her.' Florence informed Maud that the tiny winner of the very first contest in 1921 had been Miss Washington, D.C. (5'1"), named at a time when the contestants represented cities, not states. Maud early learned to listen, to nod understandingly at Florence's parade of facts and statistics, and to try to remember them, for her mother's sake.

At a time when Maud's own skin was suffering the outrages of pimples and purulent sores (and when she had begun another, hidden, indignity—this one bloody and inflicted on all young girls, her mother told her), Florence railed against the judges of the contest for allowing the contestants to describe their complexions as peachy, or creamy, instead of fair. Maud decided Florence thought these poeticisms a violation of the classic beauty of language she thought fitting for members of the pageant. So intensely did Florence believe in the validity of every aspect of the event that euphemisms offended her sense of propriety. To her the pageant was akin to church processions: holy, blessed, and full of divine grace.

During the years that Florence took her week of rest in Atlantic City, Maud stayed at home with her grouchy, silent Aunt Louise, who was afraid of young girls and therefore imposed rigid discipline upon her. When Aunt Louise died, and Maud was older, she stayed alone with her ailing father. But her knowledge of what went on in the resort city was encyclopedic. She knew how the weather had been last year for the swimsuit competition, who had won the talent show but lost out in the evening gown match. One year Florence had returned in a rage. The winner, the former Miss Connecticut, had, to her eyes, inexcusably wide hips—37½ inches—'larger than her bust, can you believe that?' To Florence, who believed that absolute symmetry was essential to beauty, it was a scandal. She wrote an indignant letter to the editor of the *Albany Times-Union*, but it was never published, an oversight that angered her even more. 'Indifference, lack of standards, that's what's the matter with the people in this country.' Three years later, Miss America, formerly Miss Philadelphia, was close to the ideal, with only one half-inch difference between her hips and bust. Her picture was tacked up over the mantel of the Noon house in New Baltimore until August of the year when it was removed in anticipation of September's new queen.

Florence's ambition was to serve a New York State pageant winner as a trainer, or even as a chaperon. She did not aspire to be a hostess. She knew she was ruled out because these were always local Atlantic City women whose favored positions raised them almost to nobility during the magic week of the pageant. Florence was consoled by knowing that, after years of devoted attendance, she was more than qualified to be a chaperon. Only reluctantly did she come to realize that such a responsibility, serving a candidate, utilized three months or more of the lucky lady's year. She would have to give up her job at the hospital, which she could not afford to do.

Always, she spoke of the candidates with familial reverence usually reserved for novices in a convent. 'You see,' she said to Maud, 'you need to start with a promising girl, working with her for a year, maybe two, before she's ready to enter. You're with her all the time while she's still in high school. Work on her, with her, teach her how to groom herself, every part, head to body, how to improve her best features and play down her less good ones, stand straight but not too straight, like military men.' She glanced at her husband, who sat still in his chair, not listening, it seemed, his mind on his tin soldiers guarding their paper terrain. 'Poise, it's called. You teach them how to be poised.'

'I thought poise was balance or equilibrium, like being poised on the edge of a cliff, like the Charlie Chaplin cabin in *The Gold Rush*, or something,' Maud said. 'Well, I suppose that too. But it also means she holds herself, her shoulders and hips and legs and arms, standing just right every time she stops moving. Stopping in just the right pose, graceful-like, all together. What the judges give points for is called "grace of bearing." '

Maud felt her own round shoulders curve in further, so that her sternum ached with pressure, a living model, she hoped, of what Miss America was not, the ugliest of ugly Miss New Baltimores, fat, short, half blind, unpoised. 'Then her clothes. It matters a lot how the swimsuit is cut for her particular figger, the color, the materials, the neckline. Then you need to worry about what your girl wears for talent night, so it shows her off well no matter what things she does, something awkward like, you know, like tap dancing or reciting Kipling's *If*. Then the most important— the evening gown. That counts for an awful lot. And the gloves . . . '

'Gloves? They wear gloves? When?' Maud asked.   'Oh my yes. With the evening gown, always. When did you think?'

Maud's fingers were so fat that they fit best into the mittens she wore until it grew warm enough to go without them. The thought of jamming her beefy hands into long white kid gloves wrinkled only at the elbow made her arms and hands ache. 'And her hair. That's probably the thing I could be best at. I've watched it being done on girls a lot. I know how to do it different every time, for every event and appearance, all week. The trainers say they "build the hair" or "construct a style." Not like I have it done, set, you know,' she said, glancing at Maud's chopped-off black hair, which tended to arrange itself into disunited strands. 'They think of it as a structure to be built on the girl's head. That's very, very important.'

Maud nodded, and pushed her oily bangs out of her eyes with the eraser end of her pencil. 'So much for structure,' she thought, and went on appearing to listen to her mother. Florence had come to think of herself as a necessary and integral part of the pageant family. It was true that she was well known at the headquarters on Tennessee Avenue and the Boardwalk. More than merely an ardent fan, she was helpful, ready at any moment to sew a strap that broke just before appearance time, to deliver a message outside the walls of the hotel where the contestants were sequestered.

Florence lectured her family about the high morality that attended the pageant. To prevent the kinds of scandals of which the hotel owners had been so fearful, the girls were not allowed to see any man, neither brother nor father, let alone a male acquaintance, during the entire week they were competing in Atlantic City. 'No talking to any man, relative or not, in case the onlookers or the judges might think they were their boyfriends, so they would begin to wonder if the girls were pure.' Florence's best moments came when she was asked by a lovesick contestant to place a telephone call out of earshot of her trainer, her chaperon or a hostess. Such a service was not against the rules. Florence carefully wrote down the message and delivered it on a Boardwalk telephone to Harvey, or Billy-Lee or Derwin, who was staying nearby in an inexpensive rooming house. Then she wrote on the back of the note the boyfriend's response, always full of tenderness, good wishes and avid mention of reunion. She enjoyed the game of reporting what he said to Miss Idaho or Miss New Mexico, at a rare moment when no one else was around.

Florence had no gift for evocative narrative. Of course, her failure mattered not at all to Joseph, who hardly listened. But Maud had to settle for statistics and the special no-menclature she was treated to: 'evening gown' always, never 'dress'; 'swimsuit' for 'bathing suit.' 'Talent' for what were performances that showed very little evidence of compe-tence. She wished her mother had been endowed with more understanding, more insight. She wanted to understand why the girls submitted themselves to the terrible rigors of the display, why the helpers devoted their lives to the enterprise. What brought thousands of spectators to Atlantic City to see the week of events? Most of all, Maud needed to know why, compulsively and totally absorbed, Florence Noon went year and year after year to witness every step of the process that led to the crowning of a Miss America.

❧

THERE ARE NO REMOTE PLACES left on this planet. Visitors, tourists, explorers, crowd into every faraway corner, creating spoilage or 'restoration,' like imitators copying old masters in museums. The old place is 'improved,' so that it becomes common, even comic. The last frontier, the only remote place, is the interior of the self. The final privacy.

Elizabeth Becker, called Liz almost from the day she was born, grew up in Greenwich Village, a cozy, narrow-streeted and alleyed area of New York City, in a small apartment on Christopher Street. She bicycled in Washington Square Park around the greened-over statue of Garibaldi, shooting marbles in the slutch around the trees with Italian kids whose fathers played checkers on the benches nearby. She jumped rope with skillful barefoot Chinese kids from Bleecker Street. When she was older, she wandered the short streets and mews that pushed off from the Square in every direction. To her satisfaction her life was perfectly haphazard, a happy characteristic she was always to attribute to never seeing anything odd about West Fourth Street and West Eleventh Street crossing each other in the Village's comfortable il-logic. To most New Yorkers, in those days, the Village was a puzzle, remote and almost unknown.

Liz's parents had once been Village bohemians, had known Maxwell Bodenheim to say hello to on Eighth Street, had hobnobbed with artists whose studios faced compulsively north as though only the light from that direction could illuminate their privileged canvases. Once, just before they were married, while they were still very good young friends, bedmates and classmates at college, Liz's parents had been invited to Friday-afternoon tea at the Bank Street apartment of Edith Lewis and Willa Cather. 'What was she like?' Liz asked, meaning the novelist whose Nebraska novels of the twenties she had read in high school. 'Very stolid. Very silent. Not interesting to me,' her father said. 'No interest at all in politics, or people, for that matter, that I could see. And that was in nineteen twenty-seven that we went, the year Nicola Sacco and Bartolomeo Vanzetti died.'

Liz admired her parents. Muriel and Marcus Becker were good-humored, gentle people who accepted the early decline in their fortunes with a stoic grace. After graduation from college—he had been a much commended political science student at City College of New York and she a history major, Phi Beta Kappa, at Hunter—they were almost instant successes. They earned their doctorates at Columbia while they taught beginning classes at New York University, he at the Heights, she at the Square. Neither of them had spent a day of their lives in a classroom beyond the environs of the city. They married at City Hall, quietly confident of their fortunes, in love with each other, their scholarly subjects, Manhattan island.

As teachers the Beckers made valiant efforts to hide their deep and growing radicalism, their belief that college teachers, like machinists and coal miners, should form unions, their convictions that Marx and Lenin were relevant to the injustices of the United States. Except for class preparations and scholarly journals in their fields, their reading matter was confined to the *New Masses*, which arrived at Two Christopher Street in plain brown wrapper, and the *Daily Worker*, which they bought on Union Square and took home wrapped in the more acceptable *New York Times*. Their admiration for Joseph Stalin and Earl Browder was undeviating. Liz, during her early, untroubled, park-green and sidewalk-gray childhood, lived with rallies, leaflets and demonstrations while her parents took her everywhere with them in the evening: to meetings where she played games with herself on a camp chair at the back of rooms in which, far up front, hung a red banner with a yellow hammer and sickle imprinted on it and beside it the American flag. While she did her homework she often looked up at the faces of martyred Tom Mooney, Earl Browder, William Foster and the Scottsboro boys. A thin, neurasthenic-looking boy named Wendell Cohen sometimes played with Liz, until Muriel said he had to go to the Saranac Lake sanitorium to be cured of his cough.

The two instructors were dismissed from their institutions in the same year, while Liz was still in grade school. It was 'the end of the term,' a phrase Liz was always to use for a catastrophic conclusion to anything in her life, although at the time it seemed bland enough. For four months they were unable to pay the rent, until Marcus at last got employment as a janitor ('maintenance worker,' he said, smiling, when anyone asked him what he did) at the tall Metropolitan Life Insurance building uptown from where they lived. Very quickly he was elected union representative. Nothing changed for Liz during that rough time. The rooted happiness of her childhood spent with two dedicated and single-minded parents who loved her went on. Their hard times were a proper part of the country's widespread depression. For a long time her unemployed mother stayed at home with her. Muriel taught her labor history, a part of American history PS 64 did not offer its students. Liz learned about the Russian Revolution, about Nikolai Lenin, Leon Trotsky and Aleksandr Kerenski, heroes and villains omitted from the public school curriculum.

Liz and Muriel walked the streets of the Village together, looking into the windows of shops that sold peasant blouses and skirts, stretched canvases and tubes of paint surrounding wood-block heads and jointed arms and hands for use as painters' models, and prints by Village artists with scenes of dark-faced longshoremen unloading immense Cunard liners, and black sharecroppers picking cotton under burning suns. At home Liz and her mother listened to records. Liz's childhood rang with workers' songs played on their wind-up Victrola. She knew who Joe Hill was before she heard about Thomas Jefferson, the Southern national hero who was never given high marks by her parents, because he was known to have owned slaves. She loved the sonorous bass of Paul Robeson, the harmonies and elevated sentiments of the Weavers, Leadbelly's gruff prison chants. To her, music was the Movement and the Party, the brave, optimistic words and pounding rhythms to which the Beckers marched on May Day. By the time she was twelve she knew all the verses of the Internationale ('Arise, you prisoners of starvation/Arise, you wretched of the earth') and most of Woody Guthrie's lyrics.

When she was very young, Liz admired her zealous parents because she thought there was no one they were afraid of. The police, pushing them away from the doors of buildings they were picketing, held no official terrors for them. They clasped arms confidently with locked-out workers and stood their ground against scabs and institutional guards. Both were often arrested. Once, when they were taken out of Washington Square Park for helping to raise a banner on the pole for the American flag saying ARMS FOR DEMOCRATIC SPAIN, a comrade (that was how he introduced himself to her and she understood at once: 'I am Marcus's friend, Comrade Earl') came to her and took her to his apartment, where, with his family, she was fed stew and milk and home-baked bread.

As she grew older, Liz discovered to her surprise that her parents' fearlessness did not extend to their own bodies. Small flaws appeared in the brave tapestry of their mutual valor. Their fears were fixed on Muriel's childbirth and Marcus's teeth. 'I will never go through it again,' Liz grew up hearing. 'They were the worst hours you could ever imagine. A breech birth, feet first. Terrible tearing. Pain, volcanic eruptions, it seemed like, for thirty-seven hours. Blood. Never again. Not for anything.' Each time Liz heard the story, a new butchery was added: 'Holes in my palms from my nails,' until Liz came to look upon giving birth as a kind of extinction, a catastrophic, long drawn out murder of the mother by the bombarding passage of the baby out of a place that ripped and bled mightily and could, with bad luck, lead to maternal death.

As for Marcus, he lived in mortal fear of the dentist. He was a private man, whose façade was brazenly, openly public. He showed his face willingly to the owners, the police, the fascist National Guard, the Klan, the Legion. But his true self was hidden. He hated to be touched by anyone he did not know and could not bear the idea of anyone examining his teeth. To him, his mouth, like other secret places in his body, was intimate and forbidden to scrutiny. 'I cannot bear to have him look into my mouth,' he told Liz. From that holy place should emerge only the sacred vocabulary of political truth, the maxims of Marx and Lenin, the saintly sayings of Stalin, and a vague, unpleasant odor of tobacco, vodka and unclean teeth. Into it went all the godly choices of his sustenance: the bread of life, and 'the wine of astonishment,' as the Psalms say. 'The soup du jour,' he would joke to his wife, 'and nothing else. No probes, no picks and axes and drills, no brushes. They all disturb the balance of nature.' Marcus never went to the dentist. His teeth turned yellow and then brown from tobacco and accumulated tartar and plaque. He believed the disturbing action of a toothpick or a brush would only activate the solid wastes that had gathered to protect his gums against infection from the outside, and the valleys and peaks of his teeth against invasion and decay. While Liz was growing up and taken to the dentist every year by her attentive mother, she watched the slow disappearance of her father's teeth. As he sat reading one of his pamphlets from International Publishers, she saw him poke into his mouth with his index finger, holding it in one place for long periods of time, moving it slightly, back and forth. He was open about what he was doing. 'I make no bones about it' was his way of transforming his dentulous act into a joke. A tooth having offended him by its weakness in its socket, he was engaged in wiggling it, in and out, around and around, one week accomplishing a small root crack, the next causing a piece to give way entirely. Then the crack, another long week of probe and shake, push and propel, until the final snap, and the tooth was out, spit into his hand, saved in an envelope marked 'Marcus's canines, bicuspids, molars and incisors.' At each extraction he would exult to Muriel and Liz, 'No expense. No pain. Even some pleasure in the process. Do-it-yourself patience and instinctive skill. That's the secret.'   'No teeth is the secret,' said Muriel.   'Well, yes. But when they're all gone, I will buy some fine, shapely, Sanforized new ones that I will clean in baking soda.'

Liz came to regard Marcus's dental cowardice as the highest form of bravery: a sacrifice of natural parts of the body in the interest of oral privacy. What could be more admirable? The ultimate defense, the preservation of one's amateur rights over one's provenance, against the professionals who are charged to do it, against the invaders. Both parents, she saw, had vowed eternal vigilance for their fears. They preserved their corporeal privacy, and had been courageous, altogether admirable and faithful, in the eyes of their child, to their intrepid tradition. Just once had her parents submitted themselves to violent extractions. Ever after, they erected effective barriers against any recurrence.

When she traveled away from the well-known and trusted environs of Christopher Street, Liz went by subway or, preferably, on the El. At fourteen she was able to move around the caverns and the air of the city as easily as a farm child in his father's barns. She knew all the subterranean passages of the IRT. Her usual journey was to Fifty-ninth Street, on the local from Sheridan Square to Fourteenth Street, then the express, which cut through the triple uptown aisles like a bullet to Forty-second Street, and then across the platform again to the local that took her to the street of the galleries. She made all these train changes without thought, her eyes often on a book she was reading.

Or she took the El. She would walk across the Village to the Third Avenue station on the uptown side, for the excitement of riding the great, rumbling uplifted iron horse of a train, on her way, via a crosstown bus, to the Metropolitan Museum of Art. Depositing her nickel into the slot, she would push, on the side marked ENTRANCE, against one of the four heavy black arms of the even-sided metal cross, and gain entry, as hard going as if she had forced the door of a vault. No sliding under the turnstile, as she had done when she was younger; it was illegal to enter so, though she was still small at fourteen and could easily have avoided the eye of the man in his cage. Once through the turnstile, especially in winter, Liz often stood at the potbellied stove the change maker kept stoked with coal. It sat just inside the swinging doors to the platform, its long, crook-neck pipe reaching to the corrugated ceiling. Her hands on the small doors to the stove, she always studied the etched glass windows, a clerestory of unexpected design that embellished the utilitarian walls. On each side of the doors hung glass-globed kerosene lamps, their wicks white and ready. Liz had never seen them lit. From her spot at the stove she listened for the train in a state of high excitement, every time, every train. She could hear it before she saw it, through the gigantic rumble of the floorboards. Then she rushed through the doors to watch its square-faced front come toward her, a lighted great eye in the center of its forehead, approaching so fast it seemed to be rammed from behind. Its tail coach was on fire, Liz used to imagine. She waited on the wooden platform, which shook as if it were afraid for its life at every approach of a train. She stood among the black-overcoated men in fedora hats, their collars turned up, their gloved hands pushed down into their pockets, and women in cloche hats over their bobbed hair, looking pin-headed after the large-hatted styles of her mother's generation.

The train paused, twitching like some malevolent bird, just long enough to take on passengers. Liz sat down and turned at once to the window as the El train began its wonderful journey uptown. Carried forward in such upraised splendor, Liz was given a view of a new level of humanity, the late-night workers climbing out of their bedclothes and their iron beds, their bare skin wrinkled from sleep. Children, leaning on pillows gray from train soot on windowsills lining the El's tracks, watched with shining eyes the passage of the train. Old men, stout, white-haired women, and slim young black men looked out, watching, Liz was sure, until the train passed them. The magnificent monster left in its wake clouds of exhaust as thick as soup, spreading over the whole of Third Avenue like an ebony seine. In the Sixties, where it made a stop, Liz often saw the same man, his face reddened with drink and sleep, the alcohol, Liz imagined, having been provided by McManus Bar and Grill handily situated below the window where he stood, pulling on his shirt to prepare for his importunate descent. In the Seventies, women were drying their clean hair in the inky air, and others, made lazy by fat, taking up their stations for the day on folded blankets, were leaning against the black grates over the bottom of their window, wires put there to protect their children from falling to the sidewalk below. In her shutter-quick glimpses of the possible comedy and drama of these lives, Liz found meat and drink for her imagination, sustenance for her growing life of amazement.

The ride uptown was a revelation for her, an epiphany, a stage on which another world existed, a lesson on how people escaped the turmoil of their rooms and themselves to look out at any view offered them for deliverance from the inside, turning away from the chatter, protestations and domestic keening, she imagined, to listen to the anonymous roaring arrivals and departures of the El. She pushed her face as close as possible to the dirty window and retreated, drawing into the privacy of her interior self the second-story level of humanity.

Because Julia Richmond High offered no art courses, Muriel had introduced Liz to the marvels of museums, and to the galleries on Fifty-seventh Street. Liz came to prefer them to the sedate and dusty rooms of the Metropolitan Museum, one opening upon the other like an endless budding organism. On Fifty-seventh Street the paintings hung in the bright rooms seemed recent, still wet, like newly hatched birds, unheralded in their shining paint, announcing unheard-of visions and uncatalogued trends. No reputations stood between Liz and the pictures she looked at. She did not need to know the painters' histories, and was therefore required to hold no opinion about what she was looking at. Her sense of freedom was immense.

One day, in the last gallery she had planned to visit, Liz came upon two rooms of non-art, as she first thought of it: photographs, mounted between unframed sheets of glass, some by a woman named Berenice Abbott she had once met at a gathering at the union hall where Abbott was photographing some old Wobblies. Her pictures were of New York City scenes, some of them in the Village. Beside them were photographs, by a man named Evans, of the dust storms then devastating the Middle West. There were gaunt midwestern faces looking out over ruined fields by a woman named Lange. As she studied the photographs, Liz felt her eyes and heart expanding at what these people had been able to see and record. 'This is an art, like painting,' she said to herself. 'Even better. Because there's no sentimentality to them, like the sweet trees of Manet or the soft Paris streets by the Impressionist painters.' All the way home she thought about the wonder of what she had seen. 'To know where to stop, what to put in and what to leave out, the right light, the proper grain of paper. How extraordinary, to be able to make these choices, with a *camera*.' Liz was struck, astonished, captivated for life.

Once, riding back down to the Village on the El, she had a sudden look into a window that flashed away behind her. But not before she saw the silhouette of a nude white man with an oversize belly ballooning out beyond his white sticklike legs and chest, his white hands on the shoulders of a black boy kneeling in front of him, the boy's mouth open to the bulbous man's pendant, as Liz had once heard it called. How was she able to see it all in that single glimpse, the high drama of a carnal moment, two actors in an exchange? Was it free? compelled? tender? violent? It became immortalized in her memory. She wished she had a record of it better than memory. How could she report to her parents exactly what she had seen, exactly as it had been, without changing it, without moral judgment, without additions or subtractions due to faulty or inadequate language, without gain or loss through the failure of her power of observation? At that moment she decided she wanted to buy a camera, and this decision changed her life.

As they grew older, Muriel and Marcus Becker began to suffer under their sense of failure. Muriel never was able to get another teaching job. When money was hard to come by, she tried for other positions without success. Marcus went to work at a second job, doing repairs on small electrical appliances, which he worked on in the kitchen at odd moments. Liz felt, when she was well into her teens, that she was no longer as important to her beloved parents. But she saw their withdrawal from her in the right light. Their inadequacy to the demands of providing for a growing girl made them cling together, consoling each other for their failings. Her response to this was a certain calculated coolness toward them masked by her understanding of their plight. After all, they had been in the world before her and probably had used up the supply of affection available to a small family. They kissed her dutifully when she said good night, but with none of the passion they seemed to reserve for each other. In her eyes they were like solitaries adrift in a world of more fortunate families. When she was younger she had wished for a brother or sister. Later she was glad she had neither, for she had come to think that the very climate of their apartment (the windows always closed against soot and head colds) would not have sustained another breathing person. Affection, like oxygen in a sick room, was meted out among the Beckers in very small doses. What there was of it, to Liz's mind, was reserved to her parents, for each other.

They were her instructors; they gave her introductions to the world of music, art, literature. They had withdrawn their early love from her in order to restock the dwindling stores of their affection for each other. So, needing warmth and creature comfort as an adolescent, Liz turned to her grandmother.

Marcus Becker's mother, Sarah, lived on the Upper West Side. To Liz that meant delicatessen odors, the vigorless steps of the elderly, the dark, promising air of movie theater lobbies and the fine, warm sweetness of Horn and Hardart, where she purchased two cupcakes—one chocolate, one orange—before she went to the Saturday matinee at the Loew's Eighty-third with her grandmother.

Sarah Becker had survived her six sisters and brothers. Now, at seventy-eight, she lived almost ninety blocks from the family of her only son, because to her the West Side of the city was a consoling and familiar element. She could not imagine leaving its boundaries to set up residence elsewhere. She never went away for a vacation; New York for her was vacation enough. The change of seasons refreshed her, the newness of bringing out, after a summer's absence, her fur coats from their hangers in the hall closet. To change her wardrobe, to uncover chairs and sofa in fall, to take up rugs and put them down again, to unhinge the drapes and then, as the gray winter blew up from the Drive making Seventy-eighth Street a tunnel of frigid air, to rehang them, pleated and pristine, taffeta and velvet protection against the coming of winter: all these rituals were vacation enough for her.

But there was more to it. Sarah Becker had always resented and feared travel. She was afraid of displacement, of losing her situation in the small area on the island of Manhattan she had taken for her own. Her parents were immigrants, bringing with them and communicating to their children dire tales of losing their goods and their houses when the cossacks put them out and burned their street down to its cobblestones. They had fled across Europe, 'never again a place to lay our heads,' Sarah remembered their telling her. They had arrived separately in New York. New York, New York: always they spoke of it as if it were an echo, a country or even a continent, and so it was to them and their many children. Not one ever moved from the borough of Manhattan. Their small business enterprises (Sarah's husband sold secondhand furniture on Columbus Avenue and died young of influenza when Marcus was a boy) and their lives stayed within walking distance of stores, movie theaters, delicatessens and the synagogue. When they prospered, as all the children seem to have done in Sarah's narratives, they moved to West End Avenue from the lesser streets near Amsterdam Avenue, as though they were crossing hemispheres, and into apartment buildings close to one another. With them came all the rich ingredients of their family lives: fervent worship limited to two days a year, horror of alcoholic drinks, profound love of food and good company in which to consume it, an unquestioning respect for education and its subsequent accomplishments, and reverence for decorous behavior, a general decency that was more immigrant and familial pride than religious morality.

Mrs. Moses Becker, as Sarah liked to be called, had been widowed for more than thirty years and was, perhaps in consequence, deeply attached to her 'widespread' family, as she called her children when she spoke of them to her friends on the benches—'widespread' because the grandchildren had moved daringly away from the hub to the south, Seventy-second Street, or north to 106th. Her deepest affection was for her son Marcus, who had against her wishes violated all the family's unwritten laws of residency and moved to Greenwich Village. Despite his nonconformity and political rebelliousness she loved his gentle spirit and way of including all humanity in his embrace. Her family was exclusive. They believed, as her husband, Moses, had always contended, that 'charity begins at home.' They gave generously to one another; they thought the rest of the world's families should do the same. Sarah never saw that Marcus was an exception to the rule. His world-hug did not include the particular, the child with the children of the world.

Liz's exclusion from his universal embrace was not known to Sarah.

Marcus and his young wife, Muriel, had left the Upper West Side after their marriage. To Sarah their departure was an emigration, a bold venture to a new and foreign land. She seldom visited them, having been south of Fifty-ninth Street only a few times in her life and north of 110th Street never. Only when the Beckers came for her to celebrate a birthday or an anniversary in their apartment did she make the long trek, and then insisted on being brought home immediately after dinner. 'Before the dark sets in,' she would say. Her children, as she continued to call them, came regularly, dutifully, in their youth, to see her, bringing her beloved little Liz for Friday night suppers. That, in Sarah's eyes, was as it should be: the young crossing oceans and continents to be united with their elders in the homeland.

Many Saturdays in her teens, after the Sabbath suppers had fallen off, Liz went by herself 'to visit with' Sarah, using the prepositional form to describe it because Sarah always said, 'I visit every day that it is good weather with my friends on the benches.' The benches were a two-block walk to Broadway from her apartment: she made it sound as if they were located in another state. After Saturday morning at the museum Liz would take the crosstown bus to Broadway to look for Sarah on the benches. They occupied the strip of sidewalk between the uptown and the downtown sides of Broadway. There Sarah sat comfortably between the two streams of traffic, talking to Mr. and Mrs. Mendelsohn, old Mrs. Kaminsky and the bachelor Mr. Stern. The five sat always in the same seats filling the bench, in the same relative positions to one another, all facing forward but each knowing, by virtue of their long association, when a remark was addressed to them. Their talk was commonplace, trivial, traditional, repetitive, but a source of pleasure to them all.

64

They brought one another up to date on the activities of their children. 'Louie goes this week to Lakewood, New Jersey, for the surgeon's convention—yes, Marcia with him. The children stay with the Laskys in their Park Avenue apartment, very nice, very big, Marcia's family is now in plastic, a new business.' 'My boy who lives in Detroit, Mortie, writes to me his wife is pregnant. Again. I wrote this morning it is time to think of what it costs to send to college so many children. Just their books and clothes . . . ' Sarah Becker's son, the apartment house janitor, and unemployed daughter-in-law, Muriel, who marched in parades and picketed at City Hall, were not fitting subjects for these exchanges of parental pride. Sarah talked mostly about her granddaughter. 'Liz knows all about the painters, from the Middle Ages and so on. A smart girl and good too, always good to me. She goes to Barnard soon.' On Saturdays her claim to Liz's affection was demonstrated when she appeared. Each time she would go through the introduction of her granddaughter to her friends, as though Liz were an unexpected, newly risen apparition. 'Oh, here now is my granddaughter Elizabeth Becker. My friends Mr. and Mrs. Mendelsohn. And here, Mr. Stern and Mrs. Kaminsky.' Liz always said how do you do politely to them all. Then Sarah allowed Liz to help her up. Together they would wait for the light that permitted them, slowly, Liz's hand under Sarah's arm, to cross Broadway to the C&L, the only restaurant Sarah ever patronized. There, Mr. Lyons, the owner and greeter, would seat them in their usual quiet corner, and they would eat hugely—blintzes stuffed with cheese and covered with lavish sour cream and overripe purple berries. Liz would have pie à la mode, and they would drink glasses of tea with lemon wedges floating at the top. Liz loved these lunches. She loved hearing her grandmother's habitual talk, compounded of memoir and current gossip. Sarah believed Liz was eager to hear about the day-to-day progress of the Mendelsohns' children, and Mrs. Lasky's unending hopes for grandchildren. Liz watched her grandmother as she talked, enjoying the play of her agreeable wrinkled face, her faded blue eyes seeming to float in their watery beds, her thin white hair floating off from her pink scalp at the least stir of air created by the ceiling fan. Separated by sixty years, grandmother and granddaughter never tried to communicate their inner lives to each other, but they rested comfortably in the currents of family, of food, and the idle talk they exchanged every week. The bond between them was strong, for they shared a religious history, if not a religion. Liz had been raised to believe that religion was the opiate of the masses, and Sarah went only on the High Holidays to worship at the synagogue. They had an unspoken sense of female alliance rooted in the patristic tradition. Sarah was unquestioning in her admiration of the girl, and Liz admired the old woman's jaunty independence, her need 'to do for myself,' as she said, her staunch determination to be alone but not lonely, her patriotism for Seventy-eighth Street, and her loyalty to her region of the city. It may be that Liz's decision to go to Barnard College, a little more than forty blocks north of her grandmother's domain, was made so that there would be no interruptions in her weekly reunions with the beloved old woman.

When it happened, she was not there to see it. She was forever grateful. It happened at twelve-twenty on a very sunny Monday on one of those rare New York City fall days when the air on Broadway is pellucid and embodies little gusts from the river smelling of honeysuckle and river damp, sweeping around the corner past the C&L to pick up smells of mustard, sauerkraut and dill pickles. The whole sweet-sour odorous meld arrived at the benches to remind the sitters that it was time to think about adjourning for lunch.

66

They had indeed decided upon it. Mr. Stern had risen and had offered his hand to Mrs. Moses Becker to make her elevation from the bench easier, when a wine-filled cab driver, Lorenzo Amati, misjudged the turn east into the intersection at Seventy-eighth Street (he claimed the bright sun blinded him), and crashed his yellow Checker cab into the five old inhabitants of the benches, cutting them down like a sharp scythe through high wheat, ending forever their years of conversation, shunting them with one fierce plunge of his blunt-nosed taxi onto the stone benches of the next world.

PART
TWO

OTTO MILE, A VISITING PROFESSOR, taught poetry at Barnard College. He was a small man with a very large, bony forehead, and wiry red hair that sprang out from his head. His hands and feet were unusually small and well shaped, appendages characteristic of a slender, delicate girl. He seemed proud of them if one could judge by the postures he assumed at the podium. The English department faculty, which had hired him with some trepidation, believed he led the poet's customarily bohemian life, but it was not so. He was a sedate man of sedate habits. He had been married for many years to a wife who cared for all his needs and was an excellent typist of his letters and manuscripts. The first financial security he had ever known was his year-to-year contract with Barnard. His livelihood had always been precarious.

Maud Noon took Otto Mile's poetry seminar twice, against the advice of the chairman of the department, who thought poetry should be studied historically, not written by students. In Maud's sophomore year, hardly knowing Otto Mile, she had blundered into his office, forgetting to knock. She found him seated at his desk, holding a mirror over his head, and applying red shoe polish to a bald area, nature and age's imposed tonsure above his halo of rusty hair. 'Get out! Get out!' he screamed. She stumbled over the doorsill as she left, feeling guilty to be in possession of the secret of a famous, vain man, and sure she would be made to pay for her knowledge during future sessions of the seminar. And so she did.

She bore his insults stolidly when she submitted some

poems. Every cruel word he said about her poetry was important to her. At seventeen she had come to college on a scholarship, knowing that she would be willing to do anything, bear anything, in order to learn to be a poet. So dedicated and driven was she that she never resented the requirements in science, mathematics, languages and history. She did very well in all of them. Her instructors did not realize that the courses in themselves meant nothing to her. She stored away what she had memorized, planning to use it all, in some transformed way, as poetic material, for metaphors, similes, images, words and phrases with the right referential value.

Very near the end of the semester, Maud read a notice on the English department bulletin board: 'Otto Mile will read his poetry at 8 P.M. on May 1 in College parlor of Barnard Hall.' She asked Minna, her roommate, if she wanted to go. But Minna, looking languorous and lovely in her long winter robe, decided she needed to read. Maud studied for her chemistry test until the last moment, and then walked across the narrow strip of campus to the hall. The parlor was almost filled, mostly with sullen-looking Columbia College boys from across Broadway. They sprawled in most of the chairs, signifying their objections to coming to Barnard (which they referred to, by a natural corruption of the name, as Barnyard) from their masculine bastion in order to hear the modern poet they most admired.

Maud took a seat at the back of the room, near one of the few Barnard girls who could spare time from last-minute cramming to attend a poetry reading. Most of the front chairs, benches and lounges, arranged in a vague semicircle for the occasion, were already taken. Maud had to push by a boy on a couch to reach the other end of it. He smiled at her apologetically—for his long legs, she assumed. But then she decided he was the sort of conceited boy who smiled automatically at girls, even girls as clearly unattractive as she was. He was good-looking and he conveyed an awareness of the fact. 'I'm Leo Luther, Columbia, junior,' he said, holding out his hand. He had to push over against his side of the couch to make room for Maud's bulky hips and considerable backside, but he seemed not to take any notice of the demand her shape made upon him. 'Call me Luther.'   'Maud Mary Noon, Barnard, sophomore. Call me Maud,' she said and shook his hand. She gave him a long look, cataloguing his curly black hair and the stiff long black eyelashes she decided should have been bestowed upon a girl. His eyes were bright black, like wet marbles. Except for them he resembled the blind-eyed, beautiful head of Brutus she had seen in the Metropolitan. Luther had a box camera in his lap. 'I hope to get some shots of him as he reads,' he said, sounding apologetic. 'But the light in here is terrible.'   She turned away to convey her opinion that this was a mindless thing to do, and fixed her eyes on the lectern set up between the long windows.

Dressed in a light sharkskin suit, white tie and white silk shirt, the poet climbed to the lectern, walking fast on the balls of his feet. His shoes and socks were white. From Maud's myopic distance he looked rather like a Christmas decoration on the Rockefeller Center tree. He pushed the lectern aside, and holding all his books under one arm, an open one in his hand, he started to read immediately. Maud forgot Leo Luther's presence beside her and never once turned toward him during the reading. Almost as intently as she watched the poet, Luther watched her, interested in the way she listened, deeply, like someone feasting after a long fast. She seemed to be satisfying a psychic thirst with Mile's rolling, musical sounds. Leo Luther, on the other hand, could not make very much of what he heard. To him Mile's poetry was an incomprehensible mixture of classical refer-

73

ences (that much he knew, but not what they meant), foreign phrases and English words whose denotations he understood only vaguely.

So interested had Luther become in the intensity of the girl beside him that he forgot to take pictures of the poet. Mile's graceful hands, his hawkish, bushy-haired, supercilious yet somehow troubled and wary look, the way his small mouth seemed to relish every word he said—all that went unrecorded by Leo Luther's idle camera.

That first evening, Luther thought Maud homely. ('Fat nose, little eyes, like beads, close together,' he was to tell a friend at his dorm at breakfast.) Oddly, she had interested him by her absorption in Otto Mile's reading. 'I will conclude by reading a few poems from my recent group of odes,' Mile said. He never looked at the audience and hardly took time to breathe between one poem and the next. When he closed the book, he clasped the volumes together under his arm and almost ran from the room, not waiting to hear the enthusiastic applause of the standing students. Maud pushed heavily past Luther without a word of apology, her buttocks almost colliding with his face. She wanted to be one of the first out of the door, before the applause started. Later she told Luther she hated the sound of applause, the sharp, mindless, often uncritical and automatic whacking of hands together, inevitable and irritating, disturbing the perfect tower of words erected by the poet's beautiful voice.

Maud's first year with Otto Mile taught her much about creative pain. He spared her no possible agony. He crumpled a sheet of her poetry and threw it across the room at the wastebasket. 'Trash! Junk! Wastepaper! Pointless. Too long. Terrible!' he shouted. After he left the room she rescued the paper ball, spread it out on a desk and reread it. Her lips formed the hard-found words with maternal compassion. She loved her own poetry, like a mother doting on a retarded child. She could easily summon up the strength to agree with Otto Mile's ejaculative condemnations, although she held to her private view that sometimes what she wrote was not so bad. She came to realize that he was often vulgar and harsh when he was discussing the work of others in the class as well. Always, she saved the rescued sheet and reworked the poem. At the end, however, she often gave in to Mile's judgment and returned the page to the wastebasket in her room.

Leo Luther sat in the lounge of Hewitt waiting for Maud to come down, wondering, to occupy the time, why he had decided to call her. Twice before, he had met her on Broadway. Once he told her he wished there'd be another reading. The first had been a milestone for him, he joked. She smiled, said, 'Yes, good-bye,' and walked on. Was he fascinated by her strange ugliness? By her appearance of sharp, almost intimidating intelligence? Was he sorry for her? Did her ugliness contrast pleasingly with what he well knew to be his own beauty? Was it his vanity that made him prefer women who seemed to admire him? He thought Maud liked him, was flattered when something he said made her smile. A smile, he was to discover, was uncommon to her heavy, almost shapeless mouth.

That evening they sat in the lounge and talked about their families, their classes, their teachers, their careers. Luther said he might like to be an actor. Maud said, 'I'm optimistic enough to think I may someday be a poet.' Luther was taking a course at the New School in documentary photography, for Columbia refused to offer anything so outlandish. He had brought a copy of *Life* magazine with him. 'My Bible,' he said. It contained pictures of the members of the Theatre Guild acting group. Maud told him she had a roommate who was a photographer. He appeared not much interested in that information. Inevitably the conversation turned to Otto Mile.

'He's a wonderful teacher,' Maud said. Luther said, 'I suppose so. But that night at his reading I thought he didn't seem to like reading much. Or maybe it was the audience he didn't like.' Maud stared at him as though he were a boor incapable of appreciating Mile's genius. 'He's different in class.' 'Nicer?' 'No, not nicer. He's never *nice* in the way you mean, not that I have ever heard. Not to anyone. But he's so amazingly acute and intelligent. With all that hatred in him for the second-rate and the pretentious, he makes you do your damndest. Better than you thought you ever could.'

Maud's face reddened. She told Luther about bringing a new poem to Mile's seminar last week. 'It was one I hesitated a long time about, because it's personal. It describes my feelings at the sight of a beautiful Greek boy's marble head, with lovely, writhing white curls and huge sightless white marble eyes. I thought of you when I wrote it,' she said and turned her red face away. Two weeks later, when they were having beers together at the Gold Rail, she read the poem to Luther. 'Do you recognize yourself?' Embarrassed, he laughed. Then, because he was touched by the excess of warmth in her words, he leaned across the table and kissed her cheek. 'That was very good. A beautiful poem. Thank you.' Maud was stunned by his gesture. She wanted to return it but could not figure how, what move to make to reach his beautiful cheek. Instead she said, 'Do you want to come to class to hear Mile tear it apart?'

On Friday, Otto Mile spent fifteen minutes hacking away, almost successfully disguising his admiration for Maud's skill. From his visitor's seat away from the table at which eight students sat, Luther watched Maud as the poet went on flaying the word structures, the feeble imagery here, the lack of central, guiding metaphor there, the weak closure. Maud sat, stone-still, taking notes and nodding. When Mile moved on to another student's work, Maud stared at her poem. Suddenly she reached forward, as if a light had been turned on somewhere behind her forehead. She crossed out a line and wrote, in her small, clear script, another over it.

In the weeks that followed, Luther usually waited at the door for the class to be over. He had no desire to sit through another painful dissection. Maud was always glum when she came out, chastened but still excited. She accepted Mile's critical lashings with outward composure, waiting for the occasional 'not bad' or, more often, 'not too terrible.' Even the customary negative forms of his responses gratified her. Once in a great while a poem of hers survived the balled-up-into-the-wastebasket fate. When this happened, Mile, anticipating the end of the period by ten minutes ('My hour consists of fifty minutes,' he had told his students the first day) would place the less-than-offensive uncrumpled poem on the table, bow to it ceremoniously, wave to the students and depart. It was clear to everyone that this back-handed act was Mile's reluctant way of expressing a favorable opinion of the work. Maud could never look at anyone as she rescued her page and put it into her notebook. She would leave the room right after Mile. On one such occasion she went past Luther without stopping. Her heart was too full, she told him later, for a word from anyone, even him. She went to her room and sat on her bed, savoring in private her small creative triumph.

Later in the semester Luther asked her if she wanted to go to the movies with him the next afternoon. She was surprised. 'The Thalia is playing Hedy Lamarr in *Ecstasy*,' Maud said. 'I've never seen her. I'd like to go.' Luther blushed and said he was in love with Hedy Lamarr. 'I've decided she is the most beautiful woman in the world. I've seen her twice in this picture already.' Maud shrugged, as though being in love, let alone in love with a movie star, were ridiculous.

They had lunch in their separate dining rooms and met afterward on the downtown corner of 116th Street. During the walk to the movie theater Luther was quiet. Maud said, 'Are you preparing to enter the presence of your beloved, like a medieval knight purifying himself for battle?' Luther walked faster, as if jokingly to demonstrate his eagerness to arrive at Ninety-fifth Street. Then he saw that it was hard for Maud to keep up. She had on the long gypsy skirt she habitually wore when she was going out. It disguised her thick, columnar legs. In it she felt both feminine and hidden. This evening she apologized for holding him up in his romantic dash to the Thalia. 'I put it on because it is almost evening and I thought it would be suitable.'

Maud wore a white puffy frilled blouse in the largest size carried in the women's section of Klein's. She wanted to look festive and 'dressy,' her mother's word for whatever was not useful and uniform. In her voluminous blouse, Maud felt her large self obscured. At a curb, when they stepped down at the same time and brushed against each other, Luther's arm touched her, and he learned that she indeed filled the blouse. Within it he sensed an enormous flood of breasts, to which, he realized, he felt oddly attracted.

In the lobby they waited for the feature to begin. The air was stale and warm. When they entered the theater they felt as if they were driving into black water. They clutched each other, like Hansel and Gretel in the forest, stumbling along until their eyes grew somewhat accustomed to the dark. They happened upon two empty seats on the side. Luther liked the feel of her dependent hand on his arm. 'In the dark there is no shape, nothing but warm flesh,' he thought. Settled down close together, behind the section cordoned off for children where the white-dressed matron sat on the aisle watching over the comings and goings of her charges, they both felt a vague content. To feel, not always to see, was a source of happiness.

For the next two hours Luther was oblivious to everything but the wondrous beauty of the woman in the movie. Hedy Lamarr floated nude in a pond, her white body enhanced by veils of hazy water clinging to it. Luther leaned forward in his seat during this scene, like the other men in the theater, as though to get closer, to be able to see her better. Then, ashamed, he sat back and reached for Maud's hand. He never took his eyes from the screen. Holding her willing hand, he watched the screen fill with the pure line of Lamarr's profile. Lamarr smiles: the even ridges at the side of her mouth look like fine lines etched on copper. Unsmilingly now, her skin returns to its unmarked, poreless perfection. Once Luther looked aside at Maud. There was no way of telling what she was thinking. He saw only her thick glasses resting heavily on the broad bridge of her nose. Was she awed at the sight of such incredible beauty, was she appalled at the comparison to her own impoverished endowments? He could not tell.

Maud thought, 'I'll never introduce him to Minna.'

Neither of them paid attention to the story. Luther knew how silly it was, and Maud was engrossed in understanding the elements of absolute feminine beauty. Years later they would, separately, remember every turn of that elegant head, every floating motion of her body in the pool, but they would have no idea of what the movie was about. When it was over they did not wait for Selected Short Subjects or Pathé News. They walked up to the Gold Rail, ordered two beers, and talked about the foolish movie, the exquisite Hedy, and photography. Luther said, 'In my aesthetics course, a fellow who likes to think he is terribly modern talks about "the cinema." He says it is a pretense at art, that "movies are vehicles, carriages, in which stars ride, not things in themselves." ' Maud said, 'That's what I dislike about movies and about photography too. They both pretend to be an art. In photographs, people, families, "sights," relatives, are so often the subjects, poised in front of vacation places and houses. Or stars say absurd things to their leading men in front of St. Peter's in Rome, like Uncle Abe in front of his new car or Cousin Lou in her communion dress in front of St. Joseph's Church in Cohoes or some such place. All of them perpetuating the unmemorable. The camera, moving or not, is too particular. It repeats the cliché with changing personnel. Art is not like that. It's general, ambiguous, suggestive, and then, if you're lucky, universal.'

Luther had no answers. He was always lost in a theoretical discussion and secretly could not see why Hedy Lamarr's ineffable presence up there needed any abstract bolstering. They went back to their dormitories. Luther's head was still filled with the movie goddess he lusted after. Yet he felt some pleasure thinking about the time he had spent beside the smart, ugly girl. Maud had said, 'I'm going to work on an idea I have for a poem.'   'About Lamarr?'
'Jesus, no. I can't say what it's about. I'll use up the idea telling you about it.'

The poem was finished in time for Mile's final seminar meeting for the year. Maud put a carbon copy of it in Luther's mailbox. On the bottom she wrote, 'Thank you for a fertile evening.' The poem was called 'The Face Within.' Maud told Luther that Otto Mile had read it aloud, not once but twice, to the eight sturdy souls who had survived his sarcasm for a year. Only at the end did she have the courage to look at the poet as he read her poem. She hated to be in the room; she knew how red and blotched her skin must be. After class she discovered she had pulled the skin from around her thumbnail so violently that blood appeared at the cuticle. Mile had said, looking at her, she thought, but was not sure, perhaps with his grudging smile, 'Well, you know, that's not too bad at all. I rather don't mind the idea of assuming that true beauty may always lie in the shallow layer under surface ugliness, the disguise, as you say, that beauty sometimes assumes to protect its fragility. Yes. I assume that's what you're suggesting here, Miss Noon?'

'Something like that,' Maud mumbled.

'I don't object to "found alive in the porous dark" and "breathing within the secret skein." '

Maud thought she would collapse in embarrassment if he did not stop quoting her words to the class. It was even possible she might fall dead on the wooden table before her, the first Barnard junior to expire in a poetry class. Looking down at her fat feet in their stretched sandals she imagined it all, and later reported it to Luther: headlines in the *Daily News*, the confusion in the autopsy room at Saint Luke's Hospital, where her body would be sent for examination to determine the cause of death. The *Columbia Spectator* would publish the results: Barnard Girl Dead from Classroom Exposure.

The day before they were to leave the dorm for summer vacation, the three friends decided to celebrate the end of exams with a dinner party. 'It's a good time for it,' Liz said, 'before we have to clean up these filthy digs.' They put together a purse of change, and Minna was sent to do the shopping. Maud volunteered to cook on the illegal hot plate, but it turned out not to be necessary. Minna came back with chop suey in three cardboard containers from the Chinese

Palace on Broadway and a cake from Horn and Hardart. Liz lit candles in two fat Chianti bottles. They put their bed pillows on the floor and sat there, eating slowly, a pace dictated by their unfamiliarity with the chopsticks that came with the food. Very hungry, they ate at first in silence, looking toward each other now and then, suggesting with meaningful glances their appreciation of the food and the company.

Maud looked at Minna, thinking how elegant were her classic features and perfect skin, how gracefully she sat, her shapely legs folded without strain in front of her, her long, sleek hair pulled back and tied with a silk scarf. Minna looked over at Liz, whose fingers were stained with some chemical she'd been using. Her hair was cut unevenly and short; she confessed she'd just given herself her summer cut. Liz watched Maud try to get her legs and large feet into a comfortable position. She herself was able to cross hers into the lotus position with ease.

Maud ate most of the chop suey. Minna picked at the crisp noodles, Liz hogged the rice, after urging it upon the others. 'Enough for everyone,' she said.   'Who says?' said Maud.   'If I'd had twice the money I'd have bought twice as much,' said Minna, affecting an aggrieved tone.   'Girls, girls,' said Liz. She cut the square orange cake into four large pieces and plopped them down on the paper plates, which were stained with mustard and soy sauce. No one seemed to mind. Minna sipped her tea and ignored the cake. Maud ate hers quickly and then inquired politely of Minna's intentions.   'You will get fat, dear,' Minna said, handing her the cake.   'I *am* fat,' said Maud, consuming the piece in three large bites. Liz ate half of hers and decided to save the rest for after the mammoth clean-up chore.

Full of food, they went on sitting, but now uncomfortably, on the floor, watching the candles sputter and melt down the sides of the wine bottles. They were enjoying the occasion. It was unusual for all three of them to be together. Maud stretched her legs out before her, barely missing a bottle. Already they were moving out and away from one another, from the messy, comfortable rooms. 'The thing about going home,' Maud said, 'is that there are enough chairs there to sit on.' 'That *is* a consideration,' said Minna. She was leaving early the next morning for a month in New Bedford, where her aunt and uncle had a summer house. She would ride horseback with her cousin, swim in the pond, read and laze in the porch swing.

Maud's spirits fell. It always happened at the thought of the long bus ride back to New Baltimore, and the end of the classes she loved. 'The house up there is too big for my mother and me. My brother and father seem still to be in it, but they don't take up any space. And I can't think of much to say to my mother. I suppose I'm lucky that I have to get a job in Ravena, so it won't be too bad.' Liz said, 'It is strange, isn't it, how it feels going home, even if I've only been ninety blocks away from the place. You feel you don't fit in the space anymore. Either it's too small, and you feel as if you'd swelled up like a sponge, or it's too big, as you say, and you can't get comfortable anywhere.' Minna said, 'You've outgrown it all, like a hermit crab with its shell, or something. People there resent that, no matter how much you try to hide it.' Liz said, 'Not a hermit crab. You're thinking of the chambered nautilus. It's an organism that grows out of one room in its shell and moves on to a larger one.' 'So,' said Maud. 'How do you know that?' 'From a poem, by Whittier or Emerson or Lowell, or one of those fellows.' Maud said, 'It's true. You grow up, and away. People in New Baltimore think I talk oddly now, *affected*, the man I worked for last summer said.'

At that moment, going home seemed a greater task for the three women than cleaning their rooms. Liz gathered up the cardboard cartons, Minna said she would wash the chopsticks and save them for next year. Maud went on sitting, reluctant to make the effort to get to her feet. With her fingers she put out the candles, enjoying the small pain the flame caused her. 'We've had a good year, all told,' she said, thinking of Otto Mile.   'So we have,' said Minna absently, already seated in her bathing suit at the edge of the sunny pond with her cousin Eleanor and the Wesleyan boys who lived down the road. Liz was quiet. She reached down to Maud and pulled hard to bring her to her feet. 'Thank you, ma'am,' said Maud, red in the face from the effort. They all stood close, looking at one another. Then Liz put her arms around Minna and Maud. 'Let's clean up the joint, as my grandmother Becker used to say, "before the dark sets in." ' The others raised their arms. They stood for a moment, locked together in an affectionate, celebratory embrace.   'As my mother would say,' said Maud, 'let's do our duty.'   Minna said, 'Yes, I suppose so. I don't know what *my* mother would say. Yes, I do. She would probably call the maid.'   'Tough,' said Liz, handing Minna the broom. The three set about their final task of the college year, removing all traces of their lives from the colorless dormitory rooms.

In Maud's senior year, after a long, hot, dull summer in New Baltimore, where she worked nights in the mushroom plant and spent her days writing, she came back to college with four long poems she thought might have some merit. She could not wait to show them to Mile in his seminar, for which she had preregistered once again in the late spring. At the first meeting he was not present. She was told he had decided he did not want to teach, and had left the faculty. A woman professor with three names and a considerable reputation in the poetics of Milton had taken his place. Most of his former students felt no sorrow at Otto Mile's departure. The brilliant poet-lecturer had insulted them, told them they lacked the grain and warp and woof for full-blooded poetry. He said they were too ignorant to use words properly, let alone originally, to create meaningful or memorable images. He had roared at them, 'What do you *know* about? Anything?' He had told them that sentimentality and the weak, easy cliché ran in their veins. They rejoiced to hear he had left, they made up rumors about the reasons for his absence, all of them insulting to his morals and the state of his mental health. But Maud was desolate. She knew he was a great poet. She knew he had been right about her, and about the would-be poets in his seminar.

Joseph Noon's career in the army, which began in World War I, when he served bravely as a young sergeant at Verdun and had been decorated twice, was ended abruptly by the disease that appeared in Maud's senior year. He had stayed in the army all his adult life because he felt comfortable in it. He liked all things military, the loose, free feel of obeying orders without recourse to the limiting exercise of free will. It was never his own choice that had taken him to installations all over the country on tours of duty. He was entirely comfortable with his bachelor's life and came home on furloughs and leaves to his wife, whose nurse's career made her the ideal wife for so solitary a man. In a way satisfactory to them both, for many years, they lived together on occasion and apart most of the time. Florence was grateful. Their infrequent sexual encounters reduced the possibility of pregnancy, she believed, after the two difficult ones she had gone through. Joseph, for his part, relished the cozy, undemanding warmth of NCO clubs and the comradeship of the dayrooms in the barracks.

Joseph's discharge came, much against his will (for once,

85

he resented 'orders') when it was discovered that he had a progressively wasting muscular disease. He was discharged, given a full disability pension and sent home to New Baltimore and to his family. Florence became his commanding officer, leading him slowly across the floor of his bedroom to his chair. He sat in the bay window watching the parade of tankers on the busy river. Their hulls rode low in the water because of the heavy load of oil they were bringing to the port of Albany. He waited, remembering their names, for them to come back down the river on their long, slow journey to New York, now seeming to skim the water with relieved grace. The burdensome cargo had been removed from their bellies. Joseph kept a tally of passing ships. He welcomed the return of the ones whose names he recognized, fantasizing that he was a lock commander, permitting their passage in the waters in front of his window, ordering their approaches, their progression through his section of river, their departure.

His deep interest, however, was in the history of the military campaigns of the Civil War. On the card table beside him he plotted the battles of Petersburg and Gettysburg, Richmond and Manassas. A contour map was draped over the table, like a limp cloth, so he was able to move only one battalion at a time, a unit symbolically represented by a single tin soldier in appropriate uniform. Studying histories, accounts, biographies that Florence brought home for him from the Albany Public Library, plotting the advances and retreats of his divisions, he was able to engage in what he had always considered the most interesting of all human activities: war. To him, peace was the lazy condition of cowardly men and now, to his great regret, invalids. In a loose-leaf notebook he took careful notes on the reasons for certain leadership decisions, the strategic causes of defeat and victory. Until the muscles in his fingers and wrists 'went back on me,' as he explained to occasional visitors, he placed his little soldiers, minute, honorable representatives of armies, in their proper stations until such time as it was historically accurate for them to advance nobly or retreat in infamy. Joseph loved the little tin men painted over with gray or blue paint and an occasional red scarf. To him they were obedient and unafraid, brave and invulnerable. Often he was tempted by their grave demeanor to have a battle go other than history had recorded, just this once, to allow the soldier in Confederate gray to survive and return to his gallant, suffering family.

In the summer before the United States entered the war, and while she was finishing her master's thesis on Yeats, Maud spent time sitting with her father, writing feverishly in a copybook on her lap. 'Why are you so anxious?' Joseph asked her once, without looking up from the hills of Richmond.   'Right now I'm working on a poem to send to my teacher, a famous poet, Otto Mile. And I'm making some notes for a thesis on another poet named Yeats.'

Her father turned to look at his daughter. 'What will you do with poetry?' As he spoke the word Maud pictured lines of rifle-bearing men, bayonets pointed forward. Suddenly they laid down their rifles and fell to the ground, wounded, defeated, and in despair in the face of such an ephemeral and countryless vacation.   'Publish it, if I'm lucky.'   Joseph said nothing. Maud watched him move a colonel around the outskirts of the city of Petersburg to outflank a general, her father explained, in order to cut off his supply lines. His silence was understandable. A man of action, he had been forced by a malignant fate into immobility and contemplation. His daughter's choice of so sedentary, so cerebral, a profession must be incomprehensible to him, Maud thought. She understood this and loved him, admiring the way he had silently consented to make do under the drastic conditions imposed upon him by his useless legs. He had delegated all activity to his tin soldiers, becoming their strategist. They moved under his stern order, demonstrating, Maud believed, how fully he had accepted the higher instructions of some divine command.

It was early evening. Maud had helped her mother prepare supper in the kitchen. While it cooked, her mother standing guardian over the erratic gas burners, Maud leaned against the arch to the living room watching her father. Even now, in his reduced state he was a fine, soldierly looking man. She moved over to his chair and stood behind him, watching him settle his men into their evening encampment at Valley Forge, his slim head, so like Spencer's, bent toward them as though to overhear their army talk. Maud wondered about his contribution to her heredity: there seemed to be an incredible chasm, a genetic misunderstanding, or perhaps a satiric contradiction between his flat, military figure and her massive, shapeless form, with breasts that reached almost to her waist and, when restrained with specially made contraptions, buttressed against her front in a ridiculous way. Bent now over his land forces, his vision was still good at sixty, while Maud's young eyes, small and myopic, were further reduced in size by her thick glasses. Wearing her glasses and looking in the mirror, she told Luther, her eyes looked like raisins. She was as short as her mother and father, but in early adolescence she had expanded far beyond Florence's tight, trim, serviceable figure and Joseph's military spareness. She could not figure out (literally, she said to Luther, making, for her, an unaccustomed, weak joke) how she had come from them. By an uncharitable Creator she had been deprived of a proper neck. Her backside took on a compensatory capaciousness to her breasts, as though some humorous god had decided to create a vertical human seesaw. In a course in anthropology that Ruth Benedict taught at Columbia, Maud learned the anatomical name for the shape of her buttocks: steatopygia. By nature, Hottentot women had the same shape. In their tribe it was no curse but a sign of female beauty. Great buttocks elongated and stretched out behind them to extraordinary lengths were regarded as highly desirable, a valuable dowry, by their suitors.

Short, nearsighted and overflowing the normal bounds of sightly flesh, Maud hated the body to which she had been assigned. Even her mouth with its broad lips was bad. 'Poor mouth,' she often called herself. Florence believed it was the result of her insistence, until she was almost six, upon keeping both her thumb and her first finger in her mouth, so long that they became sodden and bore down heavily on her lower lip. When she finally removed the water-logged thumb and finger, shamed in the presence of her first-grade classmates, Maud's lips were permanently broadened and swollen. 'It must have been habit,' she thought. 'It was clearly not heredity.'

Her room in the New Baltimore house had no mirror, a lack for which she felt gratitude as she grew up. Rarely did she look into the one in the bathroom. But in the laughing eyes and sly mouths of her high school classmates she saw some indication of what she had grown to look like. Her hair was straight and coarse; she had her mother cut it short. She combed it using only her fingers, achieving some degree of accuracy, needing no help from a mirror. Closeted and protected from her self, she forgot for long periods of time the outlandish shape that encased the poet in her.

At the end of the summer, with one excruciating bolt, Joseph Noon's heart gave out. In his useless state, needing them for everything, he had been like a slowly dying child. Seated in his chair late in the day, he dropped a soldier onto the map, gripped his chest with both weak hands, called *'Florence'* and died. Maud was upstairs packing, Florence was cooking supper: it was an off-duty night. The rush of frantic events that always follows a death in the family obliterated for them both the sorrow they felt at the sudden absence from their lives of the gentle man they had cared for and loved.

Florence was to live out her life in New Baltimore, always aware of his lingering presence in the house, her memory of him sharp, clear and painful. She came to forget his long-absent army career and believed that every day of their lives had been spent together. Maud returned to New York and relegated her beloved father to the useful fabric out of which she would make poetry.

Just before Christmas vacation, 1939, the weekend before the recess, Maud, defying all the house rules, invited Luther up to her room to see their tree. He came up when the housemother wasn't looking, sneaking up the stairs. The tree turned out to be one full branch of Northern pine stuck upright into a bed of modeling clay in a large flowerpot. It was lavishly decorated with tinsel, strung popcorn and cranberries. Luther had rushed over after class at three, pleased to be asked up. He expressed admiration for the tree. He took a snapshot of it, a shadowy Maud behind it, for she refused to allow him to come closer or to turn on extra lights. That afternoon the light outside was gray, the window frosted over after a morning ice storm. Luther was hardly able to see through the lens.

After the picture taking, Maud made coffee on Minna's illegal hot plate. They drank it in silence. Luther's head filled with the restorative fumes from the strong coffee made in a flaking, battered pot. He gathered his courage. This was the day, the time, he thought, to try. Maud had closed the door to the room, since his presence there could well get her expelled. But the act made Luther wonder if her closing the door indicated she too wanted 'to do it.'   'I have nothing else to offer you,' she said. She seemed uneasy. 'Unless you drink tea on top of coffee. I have lemon.'   'Oh no, next time maybe. Anyway, I take my tea straight.'   Maud smiled. 'In these rooms, which I share with a beautiful upper-class girl, my other roommate, Liz Becker, and I are not allowed to be so casual about tea. It's not a drink with Minna, it's a ceremony. If you don't see it through from the beginning to end you seriously affect the quality of the . . . of the "potation," I think is the word.'   'What's a potation?'   'An elaborate drink, I believe.'

They were fencing for time, not caring about what they said. 'Simple as that? Then why not say drink?'

It was a foolish question. Luther wondered why he had asked. He supposed he was feeling irritable because he didn't know how to start what he had in mind to do. Waiting for the right moment, he wondered, 'Why do I want to go to bed with her? Do I want to see her undressed, without her weird, cover-all clothes?' He decided it must be a desire to see those great breasts unbound. He was curious about how a girl so bountifully endowed with both brains and flesh would behave during the act of sex. He felt no stirrings of love for her. 'How *could* I?' he asked himself. But his curiosity suspended all logic.

Holding the cups with dregs of coffee in them, they sat, looking inquiringly at each other. Luther was trying to decide on a strategy. Having twice before had intercourse with girls he had suspected of being virgins, he knew of only two approaches: a rough, determined strategy that had succeeded well with a handsome girl in Greenwich Village, who then turned out to be far more experienced than he; and the shy, diffident non-approach that had worked with a timid girl in the choir of St. Matthew's Episcopal Church in Lincoln, Nebraska, where they were both born and raised.

But his successful advance may have frightened the little soprano, because she would never see him again. Luther debated both modes and then, fortunately, hit upon a third. He smiled his wide, Greek boy's white-toothed engaging smile and said, 'Maud, would you consider . . . ah, um, coupling with me?' *'Coupling?'* 'Yes. Well, I chose the word because it seems to go well with potation. I've finished my coffee, by the way.' 'Want some more?' 'No. No, thank you. What I'd really like is for you to take off your clothes so we can make love—that is,' he said with self-conscious hesitation, 'if you want to make love with me.'

Maud stood up. The cup rang in its saucer as she planted her feet heavily on the wooden floor. Luther felt her looking down at him but could not bring himself to look up. He felt overwhelmed by embarrassment and uncertainty. 'I would like . . . to try it,' Maud said. Luther looked up to see her staring at him. 'But I've never done it before—never been asked to, to be honest. My idea is to do it with someone— and I must admit, Luther, that I like you very much—in the dark where you—anyone—would not be able to see clearly what I look like with my clothes off. As I am. *I* know what I look like. Not much. Or maybe, too much. Not pretty.'

When she said in her artless, gravelly voice that she had feelings for him, Luther stood up and put his arms around her, feeling small, insufficient and tender toward her honesty, her unburdening. She stood stolidly and did not respond in any way. 'Was she thinking of all the light in the room?' he wondered. The shade on the window was white and porous; he could see no way of darkening the room. He debated retreat, in deference to her wishes, but he found he wanted to see what there was to see under her tentlike shirt and under the starched whatever-it-was that bound her breasts. 'I want to make love to her,' he thought, and at that moment was suddenly persuaded that he felt love for her. 'I want you,' Luther said, trying to suggest by the simplicity of the sentence that it was the inner Maud, not the envelope of flesh that he desired. This was only partly true.

Maud locked the door and pulled down the inadequate shade. They undressed. She lay on her back on the narrow bed in the alcove. There seemed to be no room beside her so Luther lay down, gently, on top of her. Thus positioned, there was no time or room for the usual preliminaries. He felt heavy and awkward, his head resting on her chest, which, to his surprise, was bony, her breasts having fallen heavily to her sides. 'I'll be gentle. Don't worry.' Maud said nothing. She shut her eyes as though she were patiently awaiting the arrival of a bullet. She put her hands on Luther's head, smoothing his curls. 'Wonderful ears,' she said.

After the first, violent, athletic, pleasureless act for Maud was over, they lay on their sides looking at each other. 'A consummation devoutly to be wished,' said Maud, grinning at Luther, who did not immediately recognize the line and thought perhaps the poet in Maud had produced it for the occasion. 'Anyone likely to come home?' Luther asked. 'No, it's a good time for this,' said Maud. 'Liz and Minna have gone out to lunch, and then to a picture taking.' There was a long pause. Then Maud said suddenly, to Luther's discomfort, 'How do I look to you?'

'What do you mean?' he asked.   Maud decided he knew what she meant. 'You know, it's strange, but I don't see my looks anymore. I've decided that no one who looks like me can live forever within sight of her own body. I have to look away, to stay curled within myself, like a fetus. From there, I imagine myself looking out of a lovely face, like Minna's, or Hedy Lamarr's.' Luther, stunned by her candor, said nothing. 'Myopia helps. My inward vision is sharpened by my failure to see out. No blurring. I look in, beyond my skin, to the beauty buried in me.' Luther stared at the blotched dormitory ceiling as she talked. He was unable to say something reassuring, to say, although he thought to say it, that he was able to see the poet within when he looked at her. His secret about her was his own. In the half hour they had been on the bed he had discovered the source of his attraction to her: he loved Maud's breasts. He felt pillowed and cherished by the formless flowing flesh, surrounded and bolstered when he gathered those monstrous yet hospitable structures into his hands and then put his head down into their damp, chasmal midst.

They both lay silent. They had tired themselves out with their first unrewarding coupling. Maud's disappointment had made her phlegmatic. Luther's renewed need died away and left him without resources. He decided on an academic subject. 'You're Professor Berry's star in that Metaphysical Poets course. You must be pleased. I envy you.'   'I don't know. He liked my second paper better than the one on Herbert. That's about the whole of it.'   'You'll probably pull an A.'   'Never. With all that work I'll be lucky to get a B minus or some such negative grade.' Luther had no more conversation to offer. He decided he had better get out of the girls' dorm and back across the street. As he got up he said, 'I enjoyed it.'   'What?'   'The sex. The beginning. Next time . . .'   'I too. You know, I suspect I care a lot for you, Luther.'   He said, 'You are a bright girl, and a good poet to wit. I care for you too.'

Maud smiled. 'My mother always used to say, "Be good, sweet maid, and let who will be clever." '   'You're a good girl too,' Luther said.   'And beautiful,' said Maud. Luther put on his pants and shirt, laced up his snow boots, kissed her cheek and said, 'And beautiful too.' He pulled on his jacket, turned the key, went out the door and crept down the stairs.

Almost eleven years to the day of that consummation, on a cold morning before Christmas, 1950, Maud woke at five from a dream in which Martha Graham or Doris Humphrey, one of those two, a pliant stick of a figure, glided across an exotic landscape spotted with alligators. Shuddering from the memory, Maud got up, closed the window upon the gray New York City air, and made her way to the bathroom, where she squatted heavily on the toilet, and then neglected to wipe herself. Brushing her teeth struck her as too much of an effort. She poured two fingers of Lavoris and moved the sweet liquid around her furry teeth with her tongue. Feeling suddenly defiant she swallowed, gagged and threw up into the toilet.

In the kitchen she sat at the table, wearing her long shapeless gray sweater over her nightgown, her feet wrapped in the bed quilt. Then she summoned up the energy to stand, opened the oven door and lit the gas. Little blasts of heat warmed her outstretched hands. Across the room stood a pleated iron radiator, stone cold. She left the door of the oven open and started to boil water for coffee on the stove's one working burner.

Usually the mailman came at nine, the high point of her mornings. He could be heard dropping letters into the slotted boxes assigned to the house's four tenants. Maud waited for the sound, drinking the acrid black coffee, eating piece after piece of toast she cooked in the oven and buttered with uncolored margarine. Her lined white pad and fountain pen sat on the knife-scarred white oilcloth that covered the table's gashes. The pad was small and came equipped with a heavy sheet of ruled paper, which she always inserted between the top sheet and the next one to give her writing a formal rectitude when she was copying over a poem. The flip-up cover said the Ace pad was intended for C O R R E S P O N D E N C E and was made of FINE-WEAVE LINEN.

Once she had purchased such a pad and then found she could write or copy on no other kind of paper. 'Disorder become order,' she told herself as she entered words on the copybook line.

When nothing came through her pen to the pad, no image, no sound from her ear of a rhythm pressing to become a line, no word around which, for no reasons, a cluster of words would form, she spent her time adding to the destruction of the oilcloth, digging the blunt point of the Waterman into it. The shiny surface peeled away under pressure, leaving bare the brown, woven backing. Occupied in this way, Maud created abstract patterns, each day's excavation adding a new area of destructive decoration until, when she took a page from her pad and put it down on the oilcloth over the design and tried to write on it, she produced a dimpled text, a nonsensical palimpsest of depth and variety.

Now she tried it. She wrote a string of words that had come to her as the pen encountered the paper: 'alone and lonely, sole and solitary, last and lasting + + +'—the pen caught in an indentation and stopped. She smiled at the barrier. 'It's a subtle form of censorship,' she said aloud. 'I'm mistaken in these words. The oilcloth freezes me into silence, blocking my prosaic passage.' She dropped the pen and stared down at her fat, extended fingers, the nails bitten to a red line below their tips, white with cold. Other obstructions besides those on the oilcloth came to her. She thought of Luther, to whom other people's words came so easily. He was what, in his craft, was called 'a quick study.' In the cold air before her she watched him toss his lovely head, hearing how the words he had learned in one reading flowed from his mouth, his charming, mobile mouth taking on, in passage, the accents of wit and intelligence not his own. Then the warm strand of air from the oven wiped him away and Maud smiled at his disappearance. 'I can't think about him anymore this morning. It makes me feel worse,' Maud said to the air. She looked back at her sheet of paper and saw that the fountain pen had expelled a blue-black blot of ink. The oilcloth had received the excess and had promoted its spread into the shape of a nigrescent mushroom. She said aloud, 'All this happening instead of poetry,' and pushed the inky paper into the oven. Slowly it heated, curled, turned in upon itself in a kind of dance of death and then burned away with a thin blue flame. Maud held her hands out to it. She took another sheet, found a place on the oilcloth that was unmarked and sat for some time, staring at the page.

Nothing came. Everything eluded her, something that happened often since she had been left alone, since the cold of this winter had reached into her bones and her mind. Six months ago—Was it only six months? she wondered— before Florence took the twins, Kenneth and Spencer, with her to New Baltimore, she had been able to listen to the boys when she searched for a word, to their unison babblings and chorusing, to pick out from their inchoate noises the sounds of a word she needed. Now the warm air, having obliterated Luther, produced the twins, her beautiful curly haired sons, standing before her in their short-legged sailor suits, a summer vision in the freezing kitchen. She could not remember the word she had been seeking. She gazed at her little boys as if she did not know them and they, in turn, said nothing and so were not the help they used to be. Now she could remember what it was she wanted from the airy twins. 'Oh yes,' she said. At once the pressing need returned. Yesterday she had begun a sonnet about the inconceivability of safety. She sought a word: 'Haven? harborage? No.' The one that hovered vaguely in her head eluded her. 'How much of all this is the pointing of one's inner ear to catch the sound of a shifty word?' Sometimes she thought she had heard it, but it was too faint to catch, to pin it to the page in a stroke, before it escaped her into the obscurant air. 'It begins with an *h*. No, perhaps an *s*? Asylum? No.' Then, with great luck it came, in a miraculous epiphany of perfection: *sanctuary*. 'Let the line proceed,' she said aloud to the heat of the oven.

Often, if her luck did not hold, Maud would resort to the battered, coverless and spineless book she had bought years before for ten cents at a Ravena library sale of damaged and discarded books. She liked owning such a third-class elderly citizen of the publishing world, a book expelled from the shelves and offered for sale, like a slave, unjacketed and bare. More than the vast word-horde of its pages, she loved the preface that told how the *Thesaurus* came to be. The original compiler, Peter Mark Roget, had died before he was able to finish the revision of his 1852 work. His son took over the work, continuing the offering of suggested pools of word choice to writers. In her edition there was an introduction by John Lewis Roget, who wrote, 'It is necessary for the compiler to steer a mean course between the dangers of being too concise on the one hand, and too diffuse on the other.'

'A mean course. Lovely.' In Maud's quest for exactitude she would come upon absorbing contradictions: 'To propugn,' wrote the grandson of Roget, 'sometimes expresses to attack, at other times to defend.'

'To propugn.' How pretty. The plucked music of the last syllable. A useful iamb with meanings so diverse it suggested within itself a world of opposites, an occasion on which the poet would be utterly puzzled yet delighted with the ambiguity.

How full. How fine to have a word that can mean its own antonym, a word to confuse the reader by its numerous possibilities, too many even to be categorized by the grandson of the first great verbal organizer, Peter Mark Roget.

'Think of the critic,' Maud said. 'Propugn, he writes in

his knowledgeable exegesis of the poet's work. Propugn is the emblem of the poet's genius, the layers of connotation embodied in his word choice. Her? Will the critic ever have occasion,' she wondered, 'to say "her" and mean poets in general? A cello word, a pungent, crafty word. A word singled out by John Mark from the millions of other words in his grandfather's word piles for special notice so that she, by pure chance, was able to find the dactylic ambiguity she was searching for, the word for something like protection. *Sanctuary.*'

This morning she searched the Book, as she always capitalized it in her mind, the way the Holy Books were signified, in vain. Nothing would serve her line, her intent. When she looked up, the little boys had gone away into the thin, high, cold air of the room. 'O Kenneth,' she said. Her sense of loss, crytallized now, made her suddenly begin to cry. She closed her eyes upon the sight of the missing twins and stopped her ears to the silence of nonsense syllables that used to race between them in an aura of complete, exclusive meaning.

In June, Florence had come down to the city on a Greyhound bus to visit them for a day or two. By evening she was thoroughly frightened by her daughter's long silences, she said, by the way Maud sat for hours without moving, her fat legs wide apart, her skirt spread between her knees like a hammock, her elbows on her knees, her eyes fixed on the floor or on a piece of white paper and an opened fountain pen. Once in a while Maud looked up at the chattering twins, whom she did not seem to see or hear.

'Maud. Listen. I'll take the kids up home for a while. It'll be nice for the summer up there. You remember. The air is better upriver. And in the fall, St. Patrick's has gotten to be a better school, I hear, at least better than the public schools. Now that I'm not working they'll be company for me.' Maud looked at her without responding. At the moment Florence made her offer Maud had been hearing a three-note melody that she was now trying to provide with syllabic content. Florence took Maud's silence to mean she was resisting the idea. 'You'll be able to work, write what it is you do, better without the worry of them.'

With her pension from the hospital and her Social Security, having just completed the necessary forty quarters 'by a hair,' as she put it, Florence had settled into her old house on the river with few regrets for the rushed, astringent world of the ward room and the barked instructions at the nurses' station. She took her customary vacation in Atlantic City with the money she saved from small economies: she patched sheets with her old uniforms, saved wrappings and string, envelopes and aluminum foil. Her diet was planned carefully so that nothing was left over too long, unused or spoiled. True, she often missed Joseph. There was no one to care for, so she served a day a week with hot lunch delivery from the Ravena Methodist Church, and carried out little errands of mercy her minister suggested to her. The Stromberg-Carlson with voluptuous shoulders, the largest piece of furniture in her living room, gave content to her evenings, but still she was often lonely. She hoped her grandchildren could come to fill the emptiness of her house. She would even be willing to forego her Atlantic City trip next year.

Now she was alarmed about Maud's state. 'There's so little food in the house, Maud. What do you all eat? What do you feed these kids? And if I lived here I would complain to the landlord about the garbage in the hall. About the water being cold all the time. The wallpaper.' Maud did not respond to Florence's litany of grievances. She was absorbed in working out the logistics of the sixth line in a tricky French meter she had decided on for a poem about

Otto Mile, who was now an inhabitant of St. Elizabeth's in Washington.

Florence felt anger, for her an unusual sentiment, rising in her throat. She decided to continue the attack, as a strategy to get her way with the children. 'You're too fat. Your heart will never carry all that weight around. You're a young girl. You don't move around enough. All that sitting you do is bad. Why don't you—' 'Take them,' Maud said. 'When I've finished this group of poems I want to write, I'll come for them.' Then she added, all she could bring herself to say, 'It's very good of you.'

'O Kenneth. O Spencer.' The boys, full of seven-year-old glee at a change, at being able to go off on a visit, helped Grandma Noon pack their clothes, two of everything in one valise, as Florence called it, kissed their motionless mother good-bye, one kiss on each cheek in well-timed unison. 'We'll go to see the caverns,' Florence told them, 'And to the Capitol, where the governor is. And now there's a submarine at the docks.' The twins looked at each other, and then responded, one after the other, with a series of scrambled syllables, what Maud, in a letter to Otto Mile, was to term, 'glib, gibbous, gorgeous glossolalia.' What they said to Maud sounded like 'Bru Thosh Mog,' and then they went out the door with their grandmother, walking in lockstep like little soldiers, speaking their private gibberish to themselves and to their grandmother.

'O Kenneth.' Maud was excluded from their close union, their incomprehensible *lingua franca*. Exactly alike in form and face, meiotic versions of their beautiful father, they seemed to Maud to be formed by a single sensibility and held together by the thread of their exclusive communications. Christened Kenneth James and Spencer John, they had reached a silent concord some time after their fourth birthday. They decided they would be called by one name, Kenneth. Both shook their heads at Spencer and warded off any further debate about their decision by refusing to answer to any other name than Kenneth. Luther accepted their decision with kindly condescension, the mild amusement of the half-day-a-week parent soon to be moving on to other amusements but at the moment enjoying his children's colorful vagaries. With the meager child and wife support he was able to provide from his acting jobs, he had bought his freedom from the insoluble problems of a strange wife and loony children. Nor did Maud ever question their choice of a common name. She had now lived alone with them for four years and had borne stolidly their lofty expulsion of her from their union since they were able to crawl toward one another.

'O Kenneth.' After a while she did not bother to keep them apart in her mind. Fortunately they were rarely sick and rarely unhappy, so practical differentiation was not necessary. But if something happened to disturb them— thunder and lightning, a bee bite, a broken toy or a lost ball, they displayed remarkably fused misery. Separate names would have not served—were, indeed, not necessary. They rarely required even the one that they held in common, for comfort or praise, for admonishment or instruction. 'O Kenneth.'

Immediately after that cold January night when Luther left to go on the road with his acting company (the twins hardly noticed his absence, and he never returned except to visit), they began to talk. Not to Maud and not the *ma-ma* syllables she was waiting to hear, although they were almost two years old, but to each other in the rich, joint gibberish they developed until they were seven and went away with

Florence. Maud believed it had become a fully developed, inflected language, full of idiomatic phrases and colloquialisms. Once in a while she thought she had caught their meaning, the way that long residence in a foreign country will allow the visitor to apprehend without effort what is being said in general. But they looked blank when she questioned them, although clearly they understood everything said to them. There was, she decided, no key to their mutual, exclusive language. The best she could do was to eavesdrop on their conversations at moments when her own linguistic resources failed her, to allow the music and unlimited choices of their invented utterances to suggest possibilities to her limited English.

Maud wrote to Otto Mile: 'They may be speaking poetry. They may be the first children to start with versification and rhyme. I wager they understand syntax and the rules of rhetoric better than I. They are natural poets while I am unnatural, or at least strained and aberrant. When school has had its destructive way with them, perhaps then they will begin to speak prose. Poor kids.'

After Florence took them to New Baltimore, Maud missed them badly at first, and then buried her need for them. Finally, she began to wonder if, like Luther, they had ever been necessary to her at all, indeed (this frightened but did not surprise her) if they had ever been there at all.

'Eleven. It must be.' Maud heard the sound of paper dropping into the metal mailboxes in the hall and the mailman's slam as he clumped up the three ice-encrusted steps to the street. If she strained she could see his legs passing her nailed-down front window. She watched until she knew she would miss meeting him. She waited until all the sounds told her the other occupants of the building who were home at this hour—the unemployed teacher, the wife of a recently discharged soldier who relished the idea of a housewife, the mother of a tiny postwar baby—had come for their mail, and gone. Still in her sacklike sweater over her nightgown and wearing an old pair of Luther's socks because she had no slippers, she unlatched her door. The lock was broken, and only the chain and round gold bar that slid into the little hole remained. She looked down the narrow hallway to be sure no one was there, and then clumped to the boxes, taking her letters from the one on which was printed LEO-POLD LUTHER—MAUD NOON. Luther's name above hers had been crossed out a long time ago.

The phone was ringing when she returned. 'Maud,' Florence said, 'The presents haven't come. The last mail just arrived.' Maud was silent. Florence said, 'What shall I tell the kids tomorrow?'   'Tell them the package must have been delayed in the mail. It'll come soon.'   'They'll be disappointed. Luther's came last week, and I've had mine for everybody since September. I bought them all in Atlantic City.'   'Yes, your package is here. I'm planning to have a party tonight and I'll open my presents then.'   'Oh, good. But I wonder what happened to the one for the kids?'   'No idea. But with all the others, they'll have enough. How are they?'   'Fine, just fine. They love it at Saint Patrick's. They're the nuns' pets. My neighbor's daughter works there and she says the sisters think the boys speak in tongues.'   'Meaning what?'   'Well, I don't know exactly. Something like a gift of the Holy Ghost, she says.'   'Judas Priest. Well, Merry Christmas. Are they around now?'   'No, they're outside playing.'   'Well, tell them Merry Christmas for me, and their presents will be coming soon. In time for the Feast of the Epi-phany.'   'What did you say?'   'Nothing. Just a joke.'

Maud hung up, hoisted herself out of her chair and went to the highboy. Two unwrapped boxes from the Parker Company lay there, ribbons and wrappings piled on top of them. 'Merry Christmas, Kenneths,' she said aloud. 'I'm one great example of motherhood.' In the kitchen she filled the kettle and turned on the gas under it. While she waited for it to boil, she explored the open shelves overhead. Near the sugar bin she found the brown paper–wrapped package from her mother. When she had made her tea with a shriveled bag she had used before, she took her cup and the package to the table. 'As good a time as any,' she said aloud, and then she laughed and said, 'Welcome to the manger.'

Under the mailing paper were red-and-white Christmas paper and a tag decorated with a reindeer. It read, 'To MAUD from her loving mother.' Maud tore the Christmas paper roughly, recognizing from its wrinkles that it had been used before. 'There's no need to hurry,' she told herself. 'There's no mystery about its contents.' It was the shape and weight of last year's present, the same one she had received every Christmas since her mother had become enamored of Miss America. Freilinger's Salt Water Taffy, each gummy piece wrapped in its own white waxed paper, the white box embossed with a garish picture of the Boardwalk, the ocean and the storefront of Freilinger's itself. Every year she had eaten the entire contents in a single, gorging day. Today she closed the box without taking a piece and put it back on the shelf.

Maybe now: the fountain pen lay opened on the table, the pad of paper beside it. She tried the pen, but the ink had dried up and it would make no mark on the paper. 'So much for that,' she said aloud to the pad. She decided to sit in Luther's place, the only upholstered chair in the apartment. She lowered herself onto what she felt to be an obstruction. 'Who's been sitting in *my* chair?' she asked herself aloud, and pulled out from under her a brown cloth-covered book. George Herbert, it said on the spine. She pulled at the ribbon some nineteenth-century publisher had inserted into the binding to help keep the place. It opened to a poem entitled *The Quidditie*. ' "Quidditie," ' Maud read. 'Quiddity from *quidditus? Quid*, what. *Quid est*, what is it.' Twice she read the poem, the second time aloud in a ranting tone. Then she thought she might give the pitted oilcloth a lecture: 'The poet addresses his God, hoping for an explanation of his gift. Some justification of him as the recipient of it, by instructing Him in what it was *not*. "My God," ' she read, ' "a verse is not a crown." The next lines are filled with what else it is not.'

Suddenly the poem failed to interest her. She took a gulp of hot tea, burning the roof of her mouth, her tongue, the skin inside her cheeks. 'God,' she said aloud. 'What next?'

She spread the five pieces of mail over the table. As she used to do for the Kenneths' amusement, she made a skyscraper profile of them and then rearranged them in the form of a train. She decided to read them in order, to stretch out the pain of contact with the rest of the human race without the added pressures of its actual presence. 'I'll start with the engine letter,' she said, 'and work my way through the train to the caboose.' The first piece of mail was without envelope, a threefold sheet of paper held together with a piece of tape. She opened it carefully, taking her time so as not to tear the sheet. It was a leaflet announcing the opening of a new gallery on Eighth Street called Ars Longa. Its first exhibit was to be a collection of photographs by Elizabeth Becker. Maud smiled at the pointlessness of sending the announcement to her: she never went to galleries and rarely left the apartment anymore. The name of the place, Liz's name connected with such a place, pained her throat. She put the sheet into the oven.

The second and third cars ('no, *letters*') she could tell were bills. Mrs. Leopold Luther and her address were covered with yellow glassine. One was a department store's stern demand for payment for a skirt she had bought last summer and never worn. Across the bottom was stamped THIRD REMINDER! Another bill was from Wanamaker's for the games she had bought as Christmas presents for the twins in November. The fourth letter was heavy. She recognized its provenance at once. It belonged to a category with which she was all too familiar. Her name was written on the envelope in her own writing, and it was her hand, she remembered, that had affixed the two three-cent stamps. Inside were used-looking sheets of paper on which were typed her poems, folded so often the creases had darkened. They had gone forth bravely in late summer and were now returned to her with the customary typed slip of rejection, come home to her from their long stay at *Poetry*. Prodigals they were, returned for mother comfort. Now they required a new envelope, a new covering letter, fresh six-cent postage. Then they would be ready for the return journey, in another direction, into another part of the publishing world. 'Tomorrow. Always tomorrow, the gallant little warriors will go forth again,' she said, and laughed aloud.

Maud riffled through the worn sheets. 'No. Not tomorrow. I'll let them rest and recuperate for a while. Anyway, there'll be no mail tomorrow. No clinks against metal. No rejected children of the pen demanding the world's attention returned with regret for lack of space or absence of talent.' For a moment she lingered over the sixth poem, the lyric she had worked on for weeks after the twins had gone. She thought of something that might . . . In a rush of sharp feeling, like a chill, she reached for her open fountain pen and tried to strike out a word and insert another. The pen was dry. 'Bunk,' she said to the page and to the arid pen. Then, as though she were obeying the instructions of a jealous and critical god, she pushed the sheets into the oven and watched them burn. They followed the usual path toward death for paper that she was familiar with: browning curling, blackening and then a descent to the bottom of the lethal space, culminating in airy gray pieces of light ash. 'Very good, Maud,' she said. 'That's the way.' Her voice sounded dry and odd. 'The way to what?' she asked herself. She could find nothing to reply.

For a long time, the fifth piece of mail lay unopened on the table. 'The dilatory caboose,' she said to the solitary rectangle, her last connection to the world before Christmas. She had placed it at the end of the train on purpose: at the lefthand upper corner it read, MILE, ST.E.,DC. 'I'll save it for tonight, the Eve of the Nativity. For my party,' she said, orating with a flourish to herself, and then warmed to the subject. 'All together, we will celebrate the time of His Life at the inn, shunted to the stable, the star ascendant, suspended like tinsel over the sheep-covered hills, the magic kings wrapped in gold, padding along the path in quilted slippers, entering the holy place by celestial navigation, warming their hands in the yellow hay.'

'Bunk,' she said.

Maud took a long dress from a pile on the floor beside her bed and went into the bathroom to put it on. Facing away from the bathroom mirror, she dropped her nightgown and the sweater at her feet and stared down at her breasts. 'Sacks,' she said. 'Garbage bags. Bilge bundles.' Shuddering, she looked away and caught sight of them in the mirror. 'I look like the Kaffir woman in that anthropology text with breasts so enormous they sink beneath her waist.' She thought of Luther's loving hands on her breasts and shook with desire. Always he had enjoyed her, she was sure of that. Then why had he left her? He once said it was queer, the way she wanted to experience everything but without passion, he thought, almost as if she wanted to know how it felt, but not to feel it. 'Your appetite is impersonal, like a scholar's. I don't think you ever get enough material. Sometimes you seem to be taking notes.' He accused her of using anything, everything, as subject matter. 'You don't live, you use life as something to be put in poems. It's the same for love. The children and I are themes for your poems.' When she told him she did love him he said he found it hard to believe. 'Your humanity is first for yourself. And then for your work. Not for us.' Maybe he was right. Had she used up her deep feelings on Spencer? There were persons, she had heard, who loved once, lost their love and ever after found it impossible to love again. Was she one? So Luther stopped loving her, stopped wanting to be comforted between her breasts, to gambol in their globular fields, as once she described it to him. 'To be loved for ugliness.' She thought of her breasts, her self—'what a perversion!' she thought beauty almost preceded her into a room. 'Beautiful women have an unearned command over us all,' Maud said to herself. 'Their luck holds: they have straight noses, thin bodies, pure eyes, curly hair. When you are like me, you come to believe at last that your very core is ugly and deformed. You have sinned against beauty by having no neck and not much of a chin. O Florence, did you assume all those Miss Americas to escape your own self, and mine?'

Looking into the mirror, she said to her reflection, 'There is a whole part of existence I shall never be able to enter into or to understand: the part that pertains to being beautiful, even pretty. That door is permanently shut to me. Intelligence will never open it, or substitute for it. I am a perfect stranger to that whole world. My fat, indelicate face and trunk and hands and feet—they rule me out, by anatomical decree.'

All afternoon she sat in the window, watching the feet and legs of passersby, feeling the cold seep in under the door and around the windows, but lacking the energy to move about, stuff the cracks, cause blood to flow in her veins. In her icy hands she held the unopened letter from Otto Mile, thinking about the poet she had not seen since his incarceration. The courts had decided he was senile and crazed, a silent loon who had, in wartime, written poems about his hatred of Jews and diatribes against his native country and its Semitic population. It was said that he stayed to himself at the hospital, was rarely heard to say a word to anyone. 'Yours is the final negativism, the ultimate denial,' she had told him in a letter. She had written to him almost every week since she discovered his address. At eccentric interludes his responses had come, once only a single letter in a year, then three in one week. He told her about the poems he was writing and translating, about what he thought of the postwar world, about his desire to be free to return to Greece, which he now considered his spiritual home. He told her what he thought of the poems she sent him. It was strange: as time passed he seemed to mellow in his views. At times he was almost admiring. For three years they had corresponded in this way. Maud saved every letter, including the envelopes in his characteristically small, unreadable handwriting and occasional bits of poetry he sent. She kept them in a three-ring binder with the Columbia University seal on the cover, the one she had bought in her freshman year to carry back and forth on the bus to Albany, when she thought the seal proclaimed her a member of the New York fraternity of the intellect.

Mile rarely described the place he was kept in, although she often questioned him: 'Are you comfortable? Warm? Do you have a quiet, private place in which to work?' He never responded to those questions. Once he wrote about finding curious small droppings in the corner of his room. 'I cannot identify them. But it is fascinating to speculate. They are not from mice, or rats. Those I would recognize. Could they be *spraints*, the leavings of an otter? Or *fewmets* (deer)? Or even *fiants*, from the fox? These excrements were once of importance, you know. Two centuries ago game-keepers and huntsmen were greatly interested in the droppings of animals in order to protect—or kill—them. To our loss, we have abandoned our concern for such artifacts. But not me: I watch everywhere for them, like the ones in my corner.'

He wrote about his rigid New England childhood, an atmosphere not unlike the one in which he now found himself imprisoned. Embedded in the description was a quatrain, which in turn contained a small piece of the *Inferno*. His letters were always the same length—one side of a single sheet of paper, single-spaced. When he came to the bottom of the page he stopped writing, leaving the sentence incomplete. Often there was no room to sign his name. So he scrawled M-I-L-E in large letters across the whole page, like an erratic artist, his canvas full of paint, who decides to use the entire face of it for his signature.

In one letter he had confessed, script somewhat smaller and more difficult to decipher than usual ('As though,' Maud thought, 'he were writing in a whisper') that he was both tone-deaf and color-blind. This disclosure excited her. She felt she was in possession of a secret of great value to future critics and scholars who would some day explicate the poetry of Otto Mile. She filed the letter away in the binder with the others, determined for the moment to keep everything sent to her in confidence for her own instruction. She understood that the extraordinary originality of his effects, the oxymorons and sledgehammer rhythms, the curious and unexpected combinations of simile and place were not always consciously contrived virtues but sometimes the results of natural defects.

Years before, when she and Luther were still together, Maud thought about writing a respectfully critical article on Mile's work for the *Partisan Review*, a quarterly that had published much of his poetry. But it was like everything else she thought she might do. She never wrote it. She could not assemble her chaotic ideas into a single thesis. Then, too, she knew she needed Mile's permission to quote from his letters, to use the wonderful sestets and occasional heroic couplets with which he decorated his prose. She shrank from asking him, for fear he would stop corresponding with her. But more than that, she doubted her capacity to judge his work. Her awe of his talent was too great and would interfere with any kind of critical posture except an unacceptably worshipful one.

From other sources she heard rumors and gossip about Mile in St. Elizabeth's. The poet's red hair had turned white; he had shaved off his beard, leaving his small, puckered, pope's nose of a chin weak and feeble-looking. He was silent and would speak to no one except his psychiatrist, whom he later accused of being a Jew and a traitor to the Massachusetts Bay Colony, of which Mile's ancestors had been members. He believed the whole staff were, indeed, Semites guilty of holding prisoner one whose natal Protestantism had founded the nation and fostered its growth. He had wordlessly befriended one guard, a large, good-natured black man who wore African shirts and jewelry. To him, it was reported, he had said one word in the last year: 'No,' and one sentence: 'Nothing that is, is true.'

Maud took the unopened letter and slit the envelope carefully with a kitchen knife. The customary single page fell out, folded in three. She opened it. Nothing. No salutation, no signature and, as they used to call it in high school business English, no body. The sheet was blank. She put it into the oven and watched it go through its dying ritual. 'The last Mile,' she said aloud to herself, putting the envelope in his handwriting into her notebook. She laughed at her bad joke. Then, surprising herself, she began to cry.

It was not until midnight in that long life in the cold

day of Maud's abbreviated existence that she decided to join the ashes of her poems and Otto Mile's blank communication, placing her head, like a penitential offering, into the red-hot purifying fumes of the gas oven.

⌾⥫⥬⌾

IN DECEMBER 1939, their senior year at Barnard, Liz took Minna to lunch in Greenwich Village. Maud, the third in their Unholy Triumvirate, as they called themselves, didn't come along. She was going to sneak her friend Luther up for tea in her room. Liz wore her usual woolen pants and seaman's blue jacket, but Minna, mindful of what her mother would say if she were there, wore a dress, a new pair of Gotham Goldstripe silk stockings with seams that ran straight on the back of her shapely legs, and her fur coat. Liz's hunger was not for food but for the familiar mews and alleys, one-block-long streets and dim shops of the Village. They went straight to MacDougal Alley and Eighth Street, where the Jumble Shop occupied the corner. 'Two maiden ladies, Miss Francis Russell and Miss Tucker, run it. I'll introduce you, if they are there.' On Eighth Street Minna felt somewhat uncomfortable, but warm, in the showy karakul coat her mother had forced on her last Christmas. People down here looked less dressed up, more like the pictures she had seen of Bolsheviks in Lenin Square in Moscow, more like Liz.

A waiter appeared at their old tavern oak table in the dark taproom. Liz piled her two Rolleiflex cameras in their black cases on the chair beside her. They ordered sandwiches and ale. Liz, feeling proudly proprietary, pointed out to Minna the Louis Bouché glass paintings on the windows to the dining room. 'If we were in there,' Liz said, pointing to the dining room, 'you would be able to see the Guy Pène du Bois murals. Beautiful stuff.'   Minna nodded without interest. 'Why is it called the Jumble Shop?' she asked.   'I think because the ladies who run it found the sign in an antique shop of that name and decided it would work as well for a restaurant.' 'It's a great place.' 'Yes. Although they don't serve Negroes. One of these days I expect to find my parents picketing outside the place.' 'Oh my,' said Minna. 'Too bad Maud couldn't come. This club sandwich is delicious.' 'Just as well. This joint is expensive and Maud eats so much. Have you noticed?' Minna said yes, she had. Liz said, 'She has a way of chewing that is almost, well, *acrobatic*. Food drops from the corner of her mouth, and then at the last moment, her tongue, like a net, reaches out to catch it and return it to her mouth. Watching her eat is a spectator sport.' Minna laughed and said, 'Yes. I've noticed.' They finished their lunch, figured the division of the bill. Liz, whose invitation it had been, discovered at the last moment that she did not have enough money to pay it all. They walked to the subway, Liz laden down with shoulder bags and cameras.

'Why the Bronx? What's in the Bronx to photograph?' Minna asked. Liz laughed. 'What a true Manhattanite you are! Do you think everything of interest in this world is on Manhattan island?' Minna said, 'Sure.' and then laughed too. 'I'm better than I used to be. I once thought you needed a visa to go to the Bronx or Queens.' Liz said, 'You'll see. It's worth the trip. He's amazing, really amazing.' 'Don't you ever want to photograph ordinary things, you know—landscapes and parties and such?' Liz said, 'No. People in groups don't interest me, or scenery, for that matter. And I don't want to waste my time on individuals who aren't interesting to me because there's nothing interesting about them.' Minna asked nothing more. Liz liked to make a mystery of the object of her journeys up and down the length of the city. When Minna had no classes that day, and was free to go with her, it was not unusual to travel one hundred blocks south for a sandwich to a place Liz liked only to retrace their steps one hundred and fifty blocks to find the new object of her interest.

On the subway they studied photographs of the Wall Street secretary and the YWCA swimming instructor who were this week's Miss Subways. *'Quelle honneur!'* said Liz. 'Do you think those two really ride the subways? I bet not. That old woman across from us, in the pink plastic cap and no teeth—*she's* a Miss Subways.'   'Or you,' Minna said. She looked at Liz's grimy wool pants, stadium coat and loafers, thinking how shocked her own mother would be if she knew Liz was not wearing stockings and a skirt under a fur coat. Liz flashed her instant smile and then withdrew it. 'Wow, you're right. Am I not.'

'The number of the apartment house is three twenty-six,' Liz said. They walked some blocks, sometimes going single-file through a narrow passage on the street, their loafers sliding on the beat-down browned-over snow. On the Grand Concourse they passed a Gristede's grocery, two meat markets, a pork store and a funeral parlor, in front of which stood a line of black-suited and -hatted men, whose eyes were fixed upon the closed doors as though they were intuitively seeing the somber service going on within. 'I ought to take some shots of them,' said Liz. She shifted the strap of the camera case to her arm.   Minna said, 'No.' 'Why not? They might enjoy a distraction. Those black hats and long overcoats, and the curls over their ears. They're wonderful, aren't they?'   'No, come on,' Minna said. 'It's not respectful.'

Three twenty-six is a squat four-story building on the corner of 148th Street. The lobby is dim and cool. An old black man with a musty, beery smell closes the elevator door behind them. They ride to the third floor in a space so close their shoulders touch. To Minna, Liz seems very excited, hardly able to wait for the elevator door to be opened. 'Third floor,' the black man in his faded brown uniform says. 'To the right.' Liz walks fast down the narrow, odorous hallway, too eager to wait for Minna. Minna says, 'Thank you,' to the elevator man and then adds, 'sir.' He grunts something and closes the door hard behind her. Liz is already at the door of 3-D, her finger on the bell, her other hand working at the zipper of a camera case. 'Wait up,' Minna says. The door is still closed when she catches up to Liz. 'No answer?' Liz looks anxious and rings again. 'What's the smell here?'' Minna asks.   'Kosher cooking.'   To Minna the smell is sour, damp, piscine. Liz's finger goes again to the bell. 'I hear someone walking in there.'   'I wish you'd let me in on what we're here for,' Minna says.   'Shhh. Someone's coming. You'll see.'

The door is opened by a short, very stout, gray-haired woman in a flowered housedress and checkered apron. Her corset can be seen under the thin materials. Only her head is exceptional. It is placed on her neck so crookedly that her nose points up and to the side. Her eyes seem permanently placed on some object above and to the right. A long bow and the ties of her apron protrude from above wide buttocks. Minna sees all this as she shuts the door behind her, because the lady has turned away and starts to walk down the hall without a greeting to either of them. The hall is dark and lined with doors that must be closets or other rooms, Minna reasons. The squat woman stops short and turns. Liz and Minna, unprepared, almost run into her. She seems to bend backward a little to look Liz in the eyes. 'You are the photographer, no? You said.'   'I am,' Liz says. She shows her the Rolleiflex already stripped of its case and ready in her hand. 'This is my friend, Minna Grant. Thank you for letting us come, Mrs. Rosen.'   'Never mind that. I did not say to come. My son it was, not me.' 'How do you do, Mrs. Rosen,' Minna says, but there is no reply. It is so dark in the hall that Minna cannot see Mrs. Rosen's eyes clearly. Only later is she able to make out that they are a cloudy gray or brown, as though she were looking through bouillon. 'He is in the sitting room. We are doing the tree.' 'The tree?' There is surprise in Liz's voice when she echoes Mrs. Rosen's statement. Minna remembers that Liz's Jewish parents have no religious convictions at all, were indeed hostile to all the trappings of Christianity or of any religion for that matter. Liz told her she had once brought home a Christmas card for her fifth-grade teacher, on whom she had a crush. Her father had made her burn it in the kitchen sink. 'The Christmas tree. Aaron always likes a tree.' Mrs. Rosen gestures for them to enter the living room. 'This is my husband, Mr. Rosen.'

Mr. Rosen is seated on the sofa. He gets up at once. He is the exact size and shape of his wife. 'He looks enough like her,' Minna thinks, 'to be her twin.' Minna says, 'How do you do?' to him while her eyes are fixed on the corner of the room. There, standing beside the tree and towering over it, his neck and head thrust forward along the ceiling, is Aaron Rosen. Minna finds herself, against her will, staring at him, unable to look away. Mr. Rosen is pumping Minna's hand, saying, 'Glad, glad, glad to see you. Come in. Come in. Come in.' Aaron, hearing his father's genial repetitions, stomps across the room, his massive feet encased in slabs of leather held together by rawhide ties. The ceiling holds his head in check, pushing it forward so that his hamlike shoulders are parallel to the pole that holds the drapes at the top of the window. The whole room, in Minna's eyes, suddenly shrinks in dimension, as if a drawstring has been pulled on a purse. Goliath, thinks Minna, a colossus. The Bronx Giant.

Liz uses flash bulbs, taking pictures of Aaron from every angle, focusing on his enormous and weak-looking hands, his knees bent a little as though to reduce the strain on his neck as it crooks at the ceiling, his overgrown nose and lower lip. The lower part of his face seems blown up to twice the normal size. It is as if his giantism had eccentrically decided to expand parts of him beyond even what might be expected of a giant. Liz asks his parents to stand beside him. Instantly they take on the look of dwarfs, his mother bending backward to look up at him at her painful cocked angle, his father staring stonily ahead at Aaron's belt. His gaze is fixed so that he seems to be wishing to cut his son down to size, for once to be able to look him in the eye at his level, to blot out the spectacle of this misbegotten mammoth.

Minna still stares at the giant. Unlike most of Liz's subjects who look into her camera with a kind of placid pride in themselves, the giant turns his head toward his parents and away from Liz, as though to indicate the blamable source of his anomalous being. His eyes, deep-set and pale, are fixed on his mother, who looks back at him, her head uplifted, her eyes full of admiration and affection. Liz holds the eye of her camera level, focusing it on Aaron's rough catcher's mitt of a hand wrapped around his cane. Mrs. Rosen notices the aim of the camera and says quickly, 'It is just for now. His feet are sore. It helps him walk. The cane is for that.' 'He can walk okay,' her husband growls, in a voice that is so low and coarse it seems made of cobblestones and ground glass. 'It steadies him, is all.' Aaron turns farther away from Liz as if to show the camera's fallibility in understanding what it sees.

Clearly still perturbed, Mrs. Rosen breaks away from the tableau. 'What are these pictures for, Miss? Not a newspaper, I am hoping.' 'Oh no, nothing like that. For myself, mostly. I'm studying photography. Still just learning, really. But if I get one that's good, I'll come back and show it to you. Give you a copy, if you want it. But I'll ask your permission to put it in a book or a show of my work someday.' 'A show?' Mrs. Rosen says, uneasily. 'I don't know about that.' 'Don't worry. They might not come out well at all. The light is not very good. But I'll let you know.'

Mr. Rosen says, 'Are you finished now?' He tells his wife to bring out the coffee and coffee cake. While Liz packs away her equipment and Minna sits on the couch with Aaron, unable to think of anything to say to him, Mr. Rosen gives what appears to Liz to be a prepared talk: 'Aaron was a fine, normal baby when he was born. He weighed seven pounds. But when he was a little boy this tumor on his gland began to grow. So he got big for a little boy and then bigger and now, like this. Maybe he is still growing.' 'How tall are you?' Liz asks Aaron. 'He is eight feet eleven inches,' says Mrs. Rosen. To Minna's discomfort, Liz goes on with her questioning, reminding Minna of Maud's relentless pursuit of information. Was she the only incurious and thus mannerly one of the three? Minna wonders. 'How much do you weigh?' Liz asks, looking up at Aaron. He speaks for the first time. His voice is high and odd, a falsetto pitch straining, it seems, out of his stump-thick neck. 'A lot,' he says. His mother adds the figures with what sounds to Minna like pride. She is demonstrating her son's excess of everything. 'Four hundred and seventy-five pounds.' The coffee cups are handed around by Mr. Rosen, who gives his son a large mug. Balanced dangerously on the edge of the saucers are thin slices of a cake that looks old to Minna. Liz gulps down her coffee in a few quick mouthfuls, and follows Mrs. Rosen into the kitchen, carrying her cup and Minna's half-filled one. 'Could you tell me how old Aaron is?' 'Twenty,' Mrs. Rosen whispers, and then she begins to cry. Tears run from the corners of her eyes and redden the lobes of her nose and her cheeks. Liz stands there helplessly, wondering what maternal spring she has touched to provoke such sadness in the giant's mother. 'The doctor says something, anything, will take him away from us soon. An infection can go all through him, maybe two years, not much more.' Mrs. Rosen runs water over the cups she takes from Liz while she cries. Liz puts a consoling hand on her shoulder. 'I'll work on the pictures quickly so you'll have one if—anything happens,' she says. Her offering feels lame and insufficient to her. She is about to say something more comforting when Mrs. Rosen turns to her suddenly, the tears stopped, and says, 'You won't show it in public, yes? He doesn't go out anymore since he got so big, so the people around don't know.' Liz hesitates for a moment and then she says, 'All right. I won't show it. I promise.'

And so the picture was fixed forever, as Liz wanted it after many trials, and as it appeared in her show at the Ars Longa a few years later, and in her book that was to make her famous. Aaron, the giant, crumpled like an accordion in order to stand in the parlor, is looking down at his parents, who reach to his waist, his face disfigured and enlarged by his acromegalic affliction, looking away from the camera as if to hide what Liz saw and caught in profile: the psychic isolation of the freak, his terrible, despairing elephantiasis of spirit. A man bigger than a Christmas tree, his cane and special shoes and bent knees and weak hands early signs of his mortality (for he died two years after Liz immortalized him).

'Thank you very much for letting us come,' Liz says to Mrs. Rosen, who accompanies them to the door.   'And thank you for the cake and coffee,' says Minna.   'You're welcome,' says Mrs. Rosen. 'Pardon Aaron for not coming to the door. He gets up hard,' she says, and closes the door behind them.

On the way home Minna was stiff and silent with resentment, although she was not sure why she felt as she did. 'Perhaps I don't believe in her promises,' she thought. Liz believed a photograph was a holy image offered to the gods of creation as evidence of the trials they had inflicted on humanity, of the wrongs these vengeful deities had done to their creatures. But Minna disliked Liz's notion that the photograph superseded the person it depicted. To Liz, the picture was better, somehow. She claimed it displayed more than the photographer had intended. It was as though the camera had a way and a will of its own and told more about the subject than the photographer could know, more than the subject wished to reveal. Her Rolleiflex was a mechanical psychologist, Freud in a small black cycloptic box. The photograph was part of human history, more important than the human being, an artifact of great value to the anthropologist, the psychologist, the archivist, the theologian.

When they got home, Liz went to her room, threw herself on her bed and was asleep at once. Minna hesitated in the doorway to Maud's room. Maud was stretched out on her bed looking at the ceiling, her face blank, the blankets pulled up to her chin. Minna asked, 'What have you been doing all afternoon?' 'Having sex,' Maud said. 'How was it?' 'It was . . . interesting.' 'That all?' 'Well, interesting and a little disturbing, like a low-grade fever, or an unexpected fall from a horse, or a short but painful tooth extraction. And you?' 'We went to see a giant in the Bronx. Liz took hundreds of pictures,' said Minna. 'Better than one word,' said Maud. 'Is he another one of her curiosities?' "Well, I wonder. At times I thought his parents were the freaks, letting her do all that and then feeding us coffee and cake as though we were benefactors. The giant seemed a column of silent sanity and normalcy. And now I think Liz is the freak, for going there laden with cameras and lenses at the ready, firing at him.

I think she was trying to make him look at her so he would know what it was she was seeing when she looked at him. Maybe not, I don't know. She promised his parents no one would see the results but then . . . who knows? It all seemed—terrible, worse than it usually is when I tag along. I've decided *I'm* the curiosity. I'm going to sleep.'

Doors closed, the three women slept and dreamed, each sealed into a private somnolent capsule of the past and the future. Maud dreamed a confused mélange of herself and Hedy Lamarr bathing in a blood-colored lake. Liz saw gross reflections of a pituitary giant in a snowbank into which she seemed to be dipping X-ray plates. Minna had a familiar dream: the Eighty-sixth Street station of the Sixth Avenue El formed itself protectively over the panel of Mr. Weisfeld's skull as it lay, abandoned and brittle on the gray sidewalk. She could see spots of chewing gum surrounding it like a black halo, she saw her mother's anxious face watching her watch it, she seemed to be seeing it all through the artificially colored bright blue water of the Salvation Army swimming pool.

❧

IN THE SEPTEMBER AFTER MAUD'S DEATH, Florence decided to take the twins with her to Atlantic City, ignoring the nuns' disapproval of their absence from school. Florence was discovering how difficult it was to keep them amused and happy, now that there was no foreseeable terminus to their care. The funeral had been attended by her and the children, Luther, and two of Florence's friends from the Albany Hospital. Florence could not find the addresses of Maud's roommates at college, and the only address she could find belonged to a man in an insane asylum. Immediately after the funeral Luther disappeared, 'to go on the road,' he told her, leaving no address. He promised to send monthly support for the children, but it never came. Florence felt the financial burden. But even more difficult for her was the twins' demands for entertainment. She was never to forgive the assiduous Sisters for their intervention in the lives of the Kenneths: they had persuaded the boys to use, on most public occasions, the English language they knew well, to save their private tongue for the endless conversations they continued between themselves. The good Sisters had effected another change in the children's demeanor by insisting that one of them (no one was quite sure if they had designated the right one) be Spencer. Now they both answered to both names but the Sisters were satisfied: there were, on the attendance rolls, two names for two boys. With this schism the boys became less tractable, more demanding, less content with their own company. Conforming obediently to the general rules of the parochial school, they lost their curious self-contained and particular identity, and became 'normal.'

In Atlantic City Kenneth and Spencer quickly grew bored with the contest that so enthralled their grandmother. They scrapped with each other during the Thursday-evening costume contest at the Music Hall, disturbed the rapt onlookers and had to be taken home. On Friday, in an act of heroism for her, Florence decided to forego the swimsuit preliminaries. She hired a taxi to drive them all to the southern end of the city to see Lucy, she told them. 'This is Margate. Lucy is here. We're almost up to her.' The twins consulted with each other in a string of syllables she took to be questions by their tone, but she could not think of a way to prepare them for the sight of Lucy. When the taxi deposited them at Lucy's gigantic right rear foor, near a door that led to her interior, they shrieked with terror. Their high screams could not be staunched and they clung to Florence as she tried to move them back to see Lucy from a little distance.

Lucy was a sixty-five-foot tin-covered and painted elephant hollowed out into many rooms and observation posts. Her legs alone stood twenty feet high and were filled, for her support, with ten-foot-thick cement. She loomed into the air like a vulgar colossus and she was topped by a decrepit howdah displaying the remains of once-bright paint. Her seventeen-foot-long ears were plastered to her enormous head, and her trunk extended thirty-six feet into a bucket of cement the size of a small reservoir. At the windows cut into her belly tourists stood looking out. The bulging portholes that were her eyes were filled with whole families staring at Atlantic City to the north, and down at Florence and the twins. Nothing Florence did could stop their screams. 'Hush. Be quiet,' she told them. 'You'll scare everyone.' They clutched each other. Their cheeks were fiery red, their beautiful black curls wet with each other's tears. Florence grew increasingly anxious. 'You'll make yourselves sick. Come on, we'll get a taxi and go back. It's only a make-believe elephant, boys.'

But to the twins, immersed in their mutual and desperate terror, it was not just an elephant. 'No, no, *no!*' they screamed. It was an incomprehensibly large, thick skyscraper in the shape of a beast, a blowup like a gargantuan balloon but thick and insecurely rooted. At any moment, it would thunder forth, stomping them with its mammoth cement toes, whipping them with its twenty-six-foot tail. It was already in motion, they just had not noticed. Lucy's bulging eyes fixed on them; she lumbered, barging along fast enough to free her trunk from its bucket and then elevating the flat slit at the tip fifty feet into the air. With one move, the twins flattened themselves on the sand, one on top of the other, believing they had been pounded into the ground and combined with the sand like runover squirrels laid out flat and ground into the gray city streets, forever one with the cement. They were Bugs Bunny leveled by an enemy, shadows pressed into the sand by the rampant Margate elephant, Lucy, never to rise again.

After they returned to New Baltimore in mid-September, Miss Alabama (weight, 119; bust, 35; waist, 24; hips, 35) having been crowned Miss America to Florence's entire approval, the twins still seemed disturbed. They both complained of left-ear aches. Florence took them to the doctor in Ravena when she found their temperatures were 102 degrees. 'Mastoiditis,' Dr. Reiner said. 'Both. They'll have to be operated on.' Florence had seen many persons with deep scars behind their ears. She was shocked that this might happen to the beautiful boys. She pleaded with the doctor. 'It's just earache. Can't you give them something?'   'No. It's more than that. Very serious. There's a lot of pus in their middle ears. Inflammation has spread to behind their middle ears. I have to take out the mastoid bone to get rid of the pus.' Their heads bound in heavy white bandages, their black curls shaved, the twins came home pale and tired from the Albany Hospital. Now there were great cavities marring the perfect shape of their small, lovely heads. They became very quiet, as though the sight of the soaring Margate elephant and the excavations they saw behind each other's ears, combined with the death of their mother and the mysterious disappearance of their father, had cured their childhood pleasure with each other and with the world outside themselves. They grew to undistinguished manhood, wore their hair long at the sides over their cavities, took care of their grandmother until she died peacefully at eighty-three, married Ravena girls from their high school class and lived on the same road in New Baltimore. They worked as foremen for the Atlantic Cement Company near Albany. When a biographer sought them out to ask what they could remember about Maud Noon, the now widely celebrated poet ('The sonorous voice of her generation,' wrote *The New York Times*'s poetry critic), they said they could remember nothing about her, and sent the researcher away.

It was true. Kenneth and Spencer Luther had forgotten the language of their childhood and with it the peculiar person who had been, far back when they were both of the same name, their mother.

Leo Luther played supporting parts in national companies of Broadway shows until he was well into his thirties. He had a few close-to-Broadway roles. But by the time his acting skill had caught up with his fading good looks he had grown too old for leading men's roles. His early handsomeness and his late talent crossed each other too far into his life. He married again, a good-looking girl from Nebraska who worked as an assistant fashion editor on a women's magazine. Inevitably the marriage was doomed by his constant traveling and her cavalier attitude toward fidelity. Alone at forty-eight, Leo Luther was finished in the theater. He had grown heavy, pasty-faced and balding. He drank too much, smoked too much and suffered from constipation and hemorrhoids. Sometimes, around holidays, he thought of looking up Florence and his sons, who he assumed still lived in New Baltimore: his memory had fixed them at seven and Florence at a vigorous fifty years or so. But the natural inertia of the underemployed kept him from making the necessary effort to telephone or travel there. A writer for *Ms.* succeeded in running him down in his undistinguished Forty-fourth Street hotel, where he worked the desk evenings for his room and paid for his food, clothing, liquor and cigarettes by doing delicate errands for other guests. He procured bottles on Sunday, girls on any night, reefers and papers of coke when he could safely find them for visitors from Kansas or Idaho. The writer wanted to know about his first marriage, what he thought about the contemporary poet, Maud Noon, whether she was 'liberated' in her thinking during the years of their marriage, what their love life had been like, why he thought she had so prematurely taken her life without leaving an explanation. To all such questions he smiled his once-beautiful smile, extinguished now by the loss of four teeth close to the front of his mouth that he never replaced, and said, 'I'm writing my autobiography. You'll have to wait until I've finished, and then read about all that.' Of course there was no truth to this. Luther never intended to write about Maud, or himself, or their miserably prosaic marriage or her inexplicable death: he understood nothing about anything that had happened to them in his lifetime. He had turned his back on all of it, wiped his memory clean of the vestigial details and lived only in the present. He died at sixty-four of cirrhosis of the liver without having contributed anything of importance to the growing literature surrounding Maud Noon except a sentence or two in her biographies, and the few memorable lines in her poetry celebrating his extraordinary beauty.

ᥫᩣ

THEIR LAST PHOTOGRAPHY TRIP TOGETHER was at Minna's suggestion. In April 1939 she saw that Liz was feeling very low. 'It's the end-of-the-term blues,' said Liz. Maud was preoccupied with Luther and her final papers, and with trying to come to terms with his suggestion that they be married in the summer and share an apartment while she went to graduate school on the generous fellowship Columbia had offered her, and he took classes at The Actors Group. Minna was going to Cornell to get her master's degree in history. But she was distracted from studying for finals by her parents' generous graduation gift of a trip to Europe.

Only Liz was without direction. Nothing of what she had learned at Barnard did she want to know more about. So she applied to a publisher she had been told specialized in art books for an advance to prepare a book of her photographs, together with an essay about her views on the subject. She needed the money to finish what she had already done and to spend a year taking more pictures. She intended, she said, to go on with her photographs of solitary people.

PROPOSAL: I want to do a book about persons who live alone all or most of their lives because of the circumstances of their birth or because they have not found a mate, a friend or a community. Such people cultivate habits to fill the space around them. They smoke, surrounding themselves with warm, dense, insulating air. They have a dog or cat with whom they converse and whose hungers, preferences, illnesses and toilet needs determine the ordering of their own lives. They talk to their potted philodendron and English ivy. Habitually they occupy the same chair in their rooms, although there may be other chairs to choose among. Their daily rituals, their protection against the void, become sacred to them. If they feel themselves close to the edge of despair, if darkness knocks against their legs, they light a cigarette, have a gin, fill the tub with bubble bath, read a romance, or a Western, or treat the cat to calf's liver.

Then there are the solitaries, who live in the exclusive society of their inner selves, often because they are curiosities to the outside world: cripples, dwarfs, giants, Siamese twins and many others. These are most interesting and frightening to me. Of course, I do not understand them. Their outlandish bodies, their frankly-presented-to-the-stare faces, tell me they want someone to know about them. Their rooms, their clothing, all these assist me with the truths I can uncover, perhaps, with a camera. I am trying to understand something about the world they have manufactured for themselves as a safeguard against intrusion by the vast universe of other persons who are not, like them, singular. When I have recorded their special being in their insulated and fragile rooms, then they will know how they look to others, for the camera eye is ordinary and commonplace, harsh and critical, exactly like the world around them. And I will know, and my viewers will understand, all for the first time. I have no interest in familiar types, in celebrities, in public figures. To photograph them is a tedious repetition of accepted and already available views. I want to know about the unknown who, curiously enough, are not invisible. Indeed it is the opposite: they are tragically open to ignorant and prurient inspection because of their abnormalities. The normal are not. My subjects are like the hermit crab before he finds his shell, the snake at the moment of shedding its skin. I want to show, not what *I* see (never enough) but what the camera sees: beyond the public vision to the interior self. I wish to understand the camera's limits when it approaches these mysteries of creation and snaps shut on them. Photography, to paraphrase Franz Kafka, is a form of prayer. I want to perform a liturgy over the unique, deformed, the grotesque, the rare. *Elizabeth Becker*

This was written, of course, not by Liz but by Maud, who had listened carefully and then formed what Liz had told her into Maud's own images and expressions. But the result was exactly as Liz expected: No publisher showed any interest in the proposal or offered her any money. So Liz was depressed. The future held no doors open to her, as it seemed to be doing for her roommates, 'not even crawl spaces, like they make for plumbers,' she said. To cheer her, Minna said, 'I have an idea. Let's try to find where Gertrude Ederle lives.' 'The Channel swimmer? Why would I be interested in her? I'd say she's pretty well forgotten now!' 'That's the pathetic side of fame,' said Minna, who had read the Liz-Maud proposal. 'It would be interesting to know what she's like now.'

Liz found the address through a friend of her father's who worked in the morgue of the *Evening Sun*. Late one morning at the end of April, Minna and Liz took the subway to Flushing, in Queens. On the way, shouting over the clangor of the train, Minna told Liz all she knew about her girlhood idol. They found the place easily on Sixtieth Road and Rego Park, a small frame house long ago painted white. Its first floor had two small windows separated by a door and was extended by a narrow wooden porch whose railing seemed frail. A low picket fence enclosed the little front yard, which was paved over with green cement. They rang the bell, and waited. 'No one seems to be home. Do you think you should have telephoned or written first?' 'No phone. I tried. But yes, maybe I should have written.'

Finally the door was opened by a slender, almost miniature woman, who said in a light voice, 'Can I help you?' Liz said, foolishly, it seemed to Minna, 'Miss Ederle?' For surely nothing short of an anatomical miracle could have reduced the powerful Channel swimmer of thirteen years before to this slip of a person. She looked at Minna and Liz and then at Liz's camera hanging from her shoulder. 'No. Miss Ederle is not available. I'm Miss Ederle's friend. I live with her and take her calls.' Liz said, 'I'm sorry to intrude. I'm Liz Becker. This is my friend, Minna Grant. We're students.' A long silence followed. Miss Ederle's friend made no move to give her name or to invite them in. This embarrassed Minna. She said lamely, 'I used to be a long-distance swimmer. In high school. We formed a Gertrude Ederle Swim Club.' The friend of Miss Ederle smiled—a sweet, small-girl's smile—at that. 'I will tell her you called to see her,' she said, and started to move from the door. She looked at Liz's camera. 'She allows no pictures.' 'Could we just meet her and tell her of our admiration?' Minna asked, now determined that Liz, in her bad mood, should not be turned away. 'Well, I will see, but I doubt . . .'

As her friend turned away, Gertrude Ederle appeared in the doorway. She was a tall, heavy woman, built like a Wagnerian soprano. Her hair was cropped close to her head like a man's. She smiled at the girls, a broad, agreeable smile that revealed perfect false teeth. 'She has not changed much,' Minna thought. She resembled the advertisements for her vaudeville appearances that Minna remembered. They introduced themselves to her and she shook their hands vigorously. They all went into a tiny living room. Gertrude Ederle sat down and indicated chairs to them. Her friend sat down beside her on the sofa. Minna waited for Liz to begin but when she said nothing, she explained about the club. The nuncupative narrative sounded silly, she thought, but Gertrude Ederle looked closely at her as she rambled on. Minna said she used to visit Ederle's father in his butcher shop on Amsterdam Avenue when she and her mother went marketing. When she stopped talking, Ederle nodded and turned to Liz, who started off, having had time to prepare her defense of her craft. She talked about why she took pictures—she made them sound like valuable natural history—and she expanded upon her hopes for her book. Gertrude Ederle transferred her close attention to Liz and, when she had finished, nodded. Encouraged, believing that she had persuaded her subject to be photographed, Liz reached for her camera and began to adjust the lens. At that moment Gertrude Ederle stood up, turned with the military precision of an about-face and, without a word, left the room. 'What's the matter? What did I say?' Liz asked Miss Ederle's friend.   'Nothing. I told you. Miss Ederle dislikes having her picture taken.'   'But she said yes when I asked her.'   'No. She said nothing. She just nodded. She didn't hear anything you said. She always nods at the end of conversations.'   'She heard nothing either of us said?' said Liz.   'Nothing. Ever since the swim, when the Channel waves beat against her head for all those hours, she has been stone-deaf.'

Numbed into silence, Liz put her camera into its case, Minna said their good-byes and thank-yous to Miss Ederle's friend and they left. 'I don't understand. Why didn't that woman tell us? Why did she let us go on and on?' Liz was angry. Rarely was she frustrated in her pursuit of a subject.   Minna said, 'She came into the room before her friend could explain, I guess. But I was glad to have seen her. She still has that powerful swimmer's body, that sweet smile. Those shoulders. But deaf. How awful.' Minna shook her head.   'She has her friend,' said Liz, wistfully.   'Yes,' said Minna, surprised. 'She has that. But it's a woman.'   'So?'   'Well, it's not the same, is it?'   Liz was silent a long time, and then she said, 'Well, now you've become a widely traveled Manhattanite. You've been to two other boroughs.'

Alone in the city during the summer of 1939, while Hitler was preparing to march into Poland, when Maud had settled into a Columbia-owned apartment with Luther and Minna had left for Ithaca to begin her graduate studies, Liz occupied her parents' flat. They had gone to visit comrades in Mamaroneck. In those months she taught herself to smoke cigarettes and developed a fondness for Murads. She looked about for subjects and found them everywhere in the city. In her parents' bathroom she developed her film until her money for supplies was almost gone. With her last rolls of film, very early one morning at the end of August, she went downtown to the Bowery, to a flophouse named the Cage Hotel she had seen once from the El. The manager, still in his pajamas, waved her away. 'Only men,' he said. 'You can't go in there.'   'Are there places for women?'   'Nope. Not that I know about.'

Liz decided to hang around outside the door over which the sign, in large block letters, said ROOMS—25¢. She watched a number of men come out, but none caught her interest until a one-legged man appeared, making his way toward the hotel. He rested on his crutches in front of Liz, grinned at her and tipped his battered fedora. 'Would you like your picture taken in front of this door?' she asked him, on an impulse.   'Why me?'   'You have a nice face,' she said.   'And great legs,' he said, and grinned again. Then he looked hard at her camera as Liz moved around him, centering his off-kilter body and lined, genial face in the doorway and then not centering it, taking it all as it came, the harsh, bedraggled, cynical-looking half leg, because he struck out the stump before him as a gesture of comedy. 'Good,' she said, when she had taken all the shots she had film for. 'Thank you very much. Can I buy you some breakfast? I haven't had any yet.'   'Thank you, ma'am. That'd be swell.'

They went into the diner a few doors down from the Cage Hotel and sat at the counter near the front. 'I'm Liz Becker,' she said, and he said, 'I'm Benny. Just Benny. I promised my ol' lady when I became a travelin' man that I would forget our name, ya know? I think I almost did.'   'A traveling man?' asked Liz. 'I knew a friend of my father's who traveled in ladies' hosiery.'   'Well, us stiffs use the word different. I mean, I'm no tramp or no bum. I was more a hobo, a travelin' man, until the train I was hopping took off my leg. Now I can't move on easy like I used to. Know about bindle stiffs?'   'No. What are they?' 'Bindle stiff is a travelin' man with a bindle—a bundle, like—who makes the hobo camps, stays a couple, three days, then moves on, like a passenger stiff who is always on the cars. I was one. I got to be real good at making mulligan stew and leaving the roots for the next stiffs. For a while back there I was called Benny Mulligan. But then a car took my leg.'

Liz ordered coffee and a roll for 5¢, the sign said. Benny apologized for his appetite and asked for bean soup, rolled oats with milk, bread on which he spread a luxurious coat of mustard ('Gives it a taste,' he told Liz) and coffee. 'I used to need three squares, but now a good one before I flop in the morning is enough.' 'Are you going to bed now?' 'Yup. I sleep days at the Cage. I like the city at night. Less crowded. Don't get pushed down so easy. Cheap, real cheap that way, half price at the Cage. Days there's no one else in there.' 'What's it like in there?' 'They got cubbyholes like, about as big as you are an' not much wider. On top they got chicken wire so guys don't climb over and steal ya stuff. They got an iron coal stove for winter. So then it's good to sleep days when you can bunk close to it. I don't like nights, because there ain't no lights in there, only in the hall at the end. Some guys stay day and night, weeks sometimes, pay the two bits then the dime for the day. They play cards an' read the paper in the hall an' drink. They don't allow no niggers in this place, so it's clean, only for the crumbs.' 'What crumbs?' 'Crumbs is, er, lice. Every place on the Bowery got them. Some flophouses give meals, they got the most. Three squares they call it but it ain't nothin' but soup and bread and coffee in paper cups and such. I like to get out, move my stump around, eat at different places, the Army down the way, the shelter, the worker place on Christie Street. No air upstairs there 'cept what's used already, you know how it is? I like the outside more. Fella tole me once it was a firetrap in there.

You get someone fergets he's lit a fag, falls asleep, you're a goner. No way down but them wooden stairs. And four floors they got in that joint.

'You live by yourself, lady?' Benny asked.   'No. I live with my parents. For the time being. But I am alone, you know how, no brothers or sisters, my friends gone off to other places.'   'No boyfriend, or mate?'   'No, nothing like that.'   'Too bad. I know how that goes. Since my wife I ain't had much company 'cept for the road kids you pick up.'   'What are road kids?'   'You know, the kids . . . the kids the jockers have for foolin' with. Pretty young kids to make you think about ya wife some. I come to like 'em, even the punks, the leftover road kids. But now with the stump they don't cotton to me. So I'm by myself now again, like before.'

Liz decided to pay and leave before she gave in to the desire to cry. She said good-bye to Benny and watched him hobble toward the hotel, his crutches making a groaning noise as he went. He turned at the door and waved. She waved back. Walking to the El she was overcome by an unnamable grief. She mourned the loneliness of everyone in the world, of all people, beginning with Benny in the Cage Hotel on the Bowery, and spreading in widening circles through the city to the people on the benches on Broadway, to the trains carrying lonely people out of the city to the suburbs, to the lonely cities of the Gulf and the plains and the other coast and the lakes. The buses and Els and subways were crowded with people trying to escape the heart of solitude to other places in which to be alone. 'And the punks, the road kids,' she thought, 'helping out for a few sweet, warm minutes the loneliest of the bindle stiffs.' Walking through the Bowery's elderly, forgotten streets, Liz thought of the book she wanted to put together, a monument, a memorial to the infinite outcasts, the birth-defected, the ones-of-a-kind, the lovers, the murderers.

For some reason, she thought of a photograph she had taken in her freshman year, a Columbia University student asleep on the steps of Butler Library, his arms outstretched in cruciform shape, his chest obscured by a yellow legal pad half-covered with writing. She waited until he woke to get his name on a permission slip. Twelve months later she saw in the *Columbia Spectator* that he had published his first novel. She telephoned him to ask if he wanted to see the picture she had taken of him. He said no. He told her there were now a lot of pictures of him, one by George Platt Lynes on his book jacket. 'You must be happy, now that you've had a great success and all.'   'I *was* happy, the first few weeks. Everybody was around here and calling me up. But now, I don't know. I feel pretty much alone now. I've started the next book, for which I got a lot of money, at least a lot for me. Now I'm scared pissless. I don't think I can do it again. I'm *sure* I won't be able to do it again.' Liz remembered murmuring something reassuring, during which he hung up. Six months later, she saw in the *Times* that he had died, by suffocation. He had put his head into a plastic bag and pulled the strings tight. His second crucifixion, Liz thought, the frightened, lonely writer who had withdrawn into the diminishing oxygen of a garment bag to avoid writing his second novel.

At the El she climbed the black metal steps slowly, noticing how specked they were with chewing gum. To-morrow she had a date to photograph a woman she had been told about who was studying to be an opera singer. She was sixty-six years old, had recently assumed a new operatic name, Marie Napoli, and had been taking singing lessons since her husband died ten years before. When Liz called, the woman sounded delighted. 'By all *means*,' she said. 'I need a picture for my recital announcement.'   'When will that be?'   'In the spring. I have rented Carnegie Hall for my debut. You are, *of course*, welcome to attend.

I'm sure I will be able to save you a pair of tickets.' Under the cover of the El station where she waited for her train, Liz thought of the wife of an American writer of popular short stories she'd heard about who decided when she was twenty-seven that she was going to be a ballerina, 'as good as Pavlova,' she said. To that end she strained every muscle in her too-old body to dance on pointe, training endlessly, two decades too late. Like Marie Napoli, bracing her aged, coarsened vocal cords against the impossibilities of an E after high C. This must be the final loneliness before death, Liz thought, the tardiness of ambition, too late for realization, just in time to harbor the delusions of talent, but too late for recognition.

At the end of the summer session in Ithaca Minna met Richard Roman in Willard Straight cafeteria. By accident they sat at the same table for hamburgers and coffee at dinnertime. Roman was heavyset and broad-shouldered. He wore a tweed suit, smoked a pipe and had capable-looking hands. His brown eyes and close-cut hair matched exactly. Horn-rimmed glasses gave him a serious, professional look. He was a premed student who had decided to spend the summer strengthening his grasp on the mysteries of neuro-anatomy.

A week after their first encounter they decided to marry, feeling they could sustain each other through Richard's year of training when he was drafted: he had a very low number. Minna wanted to be married, she was not quite certain why, unless it was that it was the next sensible step in a life that her parents had taught her should be led along acceptable and logical lines: it was expected of her. She was fearful of being left, of being alone. Richard worried that the war in Europe would soon involve the United States, so he reached out desperately for an alliance that would give him a security he was sure the army would threaten. It was extraordinary that a marriage conceived out of expedience and need should work so well. It lasted thirty-nine years and provided each of them with precisely what it was they entered into the union to obtain.

At a village bar named The Old Colon (originally Colony, but the supply of neon had burned out at the last letter), Liz met Helene Flynn, a maker of silver jewelry, an artist in miniature whose slender fingers produced earrings, bracelets and brooches. She was ten years older than Liz, a thin, pale, fragile-looking woman, quiet, self-contained and a singularly devoted lover of women. Helene asked Liz home for a nightcap at two in the morning when the proprietor of The Old Colon warned the patrons he was closing. They went to Helene's East Second Street fifth-floor cold-water flat. Liz stayed on for seven years. Into a room at the back she moved her cameras, enlarger and developing equipment. She and Helene shared a closet for their clothes. Liz supplied a sofa that her parents thought was too large for their living room. Later they bought a narrow Victorian brownstone in Brooklyn Heights. They shared an enormous canopied bed, where they unburdened to each other the chronicles of their lonely searches for love. In Helene, Liz found a passion she had sensed before only in freaks.

Maud and Luther married at City Hall after Luther was declared unfit for the draft (4F: suspicion of sexual deviation, a tribute to Luther's developing acting talent, his long hair, his unusual beauty). Their apartment was furnished from the Harlem Salvation Army, but it was so small that they moved again when Maud became, by accident, pregnant and was told she would have twins. The three roommates, survivors of their separate girlhood lonelinesses, solitaries living together under the gabled Hewitt Hall roof, were now, like circus performers, partnered. They stood, precariously balanced on barebacked horses as the steeds plunged ahead into the perilous circles of the main arena.

PART
THREE

THE TRIP FROM EAST TO MIDDLE WEST would take two days, more or less, Minna had figured. She expected to take her time, to stop along Route 70 when she was tired, at some place with a pool so she could swim, rest in a deck chair, eat the expectedly poor but filling meal in a motel restaurant and sleep deeply until light appeared. Then she would head west again. In the sixty years of her life she had never crossed the Mississippi River except to fly over it at thirty-three thousand feet. She had looked down at the thin ribbon of historic mud at St. Louis, on her way to meetings of the American Historical Society on the other coast. She knew the whole country only from the air, viewing from a great height cities of the Atlantic, the Pacific, the Great Lakes and the Gulf of Mexico, all separated by thousands of miles of aerial plains and mountain ranges, deserts and farms. For the first time she would see the continent from the ground, the trunks of trees, the tassels that decorated cornstalks, the little towns that had been mere dots in her airborne trips, the human and animal populations of farms and ranches. The prairie, she knew, was gone, cut away by deep-tongued plows to reach the farmer's topsoil. She expected to see cities rising up from the plains, shining in profile against the big sky, and lakes, rivers, ponds and silver silos she knew only from photographs in *Life* and paintings by Grant Wood.

She decided it would be good to make a very early start out of the city. At five she walked to the all-night garage, paid her bill and drove the sound little Volkswagen to the side door of her apartment house. Her suitcases, book boxes, garment bags, stereo equipment and typewriter were piled just inside the door, guarded by the sleepy super, who for a ten-dollar tip had agreed to stay with the stuff until she got back with the car. 'Take care, Mrs. Roman. That's a long trip you've got. To Ohio, is it?'   'No, Iowa,' Minna said, noting the common confusion of New Yorkers about states any distance from their own. The fellow at the gas station who had filled her tank and checked the Bug for filters, belts and the other mysterious parts of the little car had said, 'Idaho, did you say you were going?'

The farewell to Richard last night was strained but not unpleasant. She thought about it as she drove down Ninth Avenue to the Lincoln Tunnel. She had tried to suggest nothing final. It was to be a semester of new pursuits, she said, a variation on her usual enterprises, a time-being away for renewal purposes after thirty-nine years of always being together. Richard had early-morning surgery today. His habit was to rise at six, prepare his own breakfast, smoke a pipe and leave silently, his whole attention fixed on the case of the patient waiting for him in the operating room. They kissed and said good night and good-bye. She said she would call on the weekend. He said, 'Not until then? How about when you arrive?' She said she had no idea when that would be. He said, 'Okay. I'll wait to hear from you on the weekend then.' The patience in his voice made Minna realize he had no idea of her intentions. He went to his room, she to hers; she settled down to an almost sleepless night. The excitement she felt, the curious absence of her lifelong anxiety about new places, the longing to be gone, the restlessness that made her arms and legs ache, kept her awake until her alarm went off, unnecessarily, at a quarter to five. Trying to make no noise, she went hastily through her usual morning ritual. Then, carrying her purse and shoes in one hand, her keys and clutch of Triple A maps in the other, she went out of 4-D, locked the door behind her and, for a reason she never after was able to understand, walked carefully down the three flights to the lobby. Was there something surreptitious and therefore illegal in that exit? Was she starting to introduce irregularity into a life of fears and habit, this early in the morning, this early in the trip, this early in her new life? The Beresford apartment house, her gray fortress for seventeen years, looked solid and ineluctable in the small light of dawn. The sun was still anchored at the East River and had only suggested itself to Central Park. She thought she ought to make an obeisance to the Reservoir, to the transverse at Eighty-sixth Street. And yes, in the direction of The Rocks. A ceremony, a ritual of departure was suitable at this moment, now that she felt certain that she was never coming back.

The city seemed somnolent, as if the current to all its usual activity had been turned off and a heavy gray skin pulled down over its sharp towers and lumpy brownstones. She left Manhattan through the Lincoln Tunnel. She had the tiled, damp passageway almost to herself. The heavily laden Bug moved along at a good pace, a spry, always youthful-seeming machine unchallenged at this early hour by heavier traffic. 'Such a car is a miracle of the imagination, the perfect escape vehicle, matching in size and intention the act I am performing. Another miracle is this tunnel,' she said aloud to herself. 'Think of being able to cross a river's bottom and still remain untouched by water. It is the twentieth century's version of the biblical miracle, Moses providing the Israelites with dry passage through the Red Sea.'

On the Jersey side she followed the signs to the turnpike. Over her shoulder she caught quick takes of a pure light rising over the towers of Manhattan, rendering the now-distant city shadowy, legendary, ephemeral. It was fading from her life, the city that had conceived, formed, bred, raised her and educated her in the sharp pleasures of metropolitan existence. Minna found it hard to bid New York farewell, harder than it was last night with Richard . . . somehow. To believe that, after a lifetime of close association with its graceless grandeur, its fitful terrors and constant excitements, she would be gone from it, for who knows how long. The offer to teach at the university in Iowa City, to help with the establishment of a section in the history department devoted to exploring the lives of pioneer women, came to her at a time when the bonds of her marriage, her motherhood, her long-tenured teaching, as if loosened by some fortuitous hand of fate, had suddenly given way. Driving down the long, uninteresting Jersey terrain, she thought about her marriage, smiling at the similarity of the two landscapes. Marriage had not so much failed after thirty-nine years as it had dwindled in force, its fibers slackened by the wasting disease of time. One after the other, the sinews had softened until, after Grant's death, everything slid away, unnoticed, into domestic oblivion. It seemed to her now to be over.

'I will not go back over all that now,' she told herself, 'until I've got all this toll stuff in hand.' She commended herself for having enough singles and change on the seat beside her. 'Housewifely,' she thought. For more than an hour, she drove almost mindlessly. Then she pulled into the Walt Whitman rest area, and fought couples and families for a seat at the counter. 'Coffee and an English muffin,' she told the waitress, whose hair was swept upward, defying gravity, to form a lyre-shaped structure. 'Wired?' Minna wondered.   'That all? No juice?' said the waitress, who was chewing gum hard.   'No, no juice, thank you.' The waitress slapped the check down in front of

Minna and went to get the coffee. The English muffin turned out to be a kind Minna had never before encountered, flat, half-cooked and tasteless, but, because she felt she had annoyed the waitress with the smallness of her order, she ate it dutifully to avoid further offense. 'There is no easy peace between strangers,' she thought, 'even on the Jersey Turnpike.'

Minna made the turns and descent into the Pennsylvania Turnpike, a road much disparaged by her advisors in the history department when she was planning her trip. It was indeed, she found, narrow, rumbling with trucks and semi-trailers, a threat at every moment to her puny Bug. By now weariness had settled on her shoulders, in the bones of her hands that gripped the wheel as the great trucks bore down behind her and beside her, in her foot on the accelerator. But she determined to go on, to get there fast, or perhaps, it was that she was determined to leave the past behind quickly. She practiced pushing back the mortal scenes of recent months, stuffing them behind the memories of Grant's golden childhood, Richard's rise to medical success, her own minor but steady journey up through the ranks to full professor and tenure at Brooklyn College. Why could she not keep her mind on all the achievements that had punctuated their lives? But no: inexorably, the events of the terrible weekend intruded themselves upon her determined concentration on the road.

A semitrailer, three car lengths long, passed her, occupying, she thought, more than its share of the lanes, forcing the Bug close to the rail, just as she began her compulsive, unavoidable rehearsal. It had been a Thursday . . . no, Friday, it must have been, when Grant called to say he was coming down from Millwood for a short visit. 'I won't stay long, don't worry.'   'Wonderful,' she said. 'Will Lois

and the children be coming with you?'   'No, just me.'
He sounded odd, she thought, as if the idea of a visit to
the city he had always disliked and to his parents, whom
he had only tolerated in his growing years, was more complex than the mere announcement of it to her.

The dinner with Grant on Friday night had been unset-
tling. Richard did not get home until she and Grant had
finished eating and after Grant had said, slowly and almost
reluctantly, 'My news is, Lois has left me. She's taken the
kids and gone to live with John Lawrence on his island in
Maine.'   'John Lawrence, that friend of yours from Brown,
the fellow who plays in rock bands?'   'That's the
one.'   'How long has she known him?'   'Oh, a long
time. When I got back from Vietnam he was always around
the house. But Lois told me it was all over between them,
and he disappeared, went on tour with Don McLean. John
was at our wedding. He's Johnny's godfather.' Grant blushed,
remembering, she thought, that his parents had not been
invited to their wedding at Cornell because it took place so
fast—and of necessity.   'I see. I gather it wasn't all
over.'   Grant shook his head.   'Poor boy,' Minna
thought. Lois was his high school classmate at Horace Mann.
He had loved one girl in his life, Lois Lehmann. His devotion
to her was absolute, undeviating, eternal, in the way that
modern love rarely is, a kind of medieval devotion that took
its impetus from Petrarch and Dante. All through his college
years he had gone on loving her, never allowing the drive
between Brown and Connecticut College to deter him. He
traveled to her college for every function to which men were
invited. He asked her to Brown for parties, weekends, games,
plays. In summers he applied for jobs at the camps in which
she was the swimming counselor. One summer, unable to
get anything else, he worked in the camp kitchen, cleaning
up the mess hall after the campers so he could be near her.
That summer, Minna remembered, Lois was head of the

waterfront, much admired by everyone. It almost drove Grant crazy, hanging around at the edge of her circle of followers. It broke his heart when she would not marry him before he knew he was to be sent to Vietnam. Lois was always a hard girl to pin down. He wrote her daily. Minna knew this because she called Lois now and then in Boston, where she was teaching public school, to find out how Grant was. Rarely did he write to them. Lois was a golden girl: small, lean, blue-eyed, charming, with a low, suggestive voice and a high, delicate giggle. It was not with money, like Daisy Buchanan's, that Lois's voice rang, but with sexual promise. Grant had been hearing that laugh and laughing with it and longing for that girl since he was fourteen years old.

'What will you do now?'   'I don't know. I can't think about anything but getting her back. I haven't been to work in three days.'   'What about the children?'   'The children—well, I don't want them without her.' Minna, who hardly knew the boy and his three-year-old sister, whom they had named, to her horror, Lolita, was appalled at his indifference to the children. He seemed to sense her feeling. 'What I mean is, nothing matters to me but her. If I can't have her, I don't want anything.' Grant went to bed early. With no practice in communication in the last years, they had nothing more they could think of to say to one another. He slept on the daybed in his old room, which was now Richard's study. Minna told Richard the news when he came home, weary but immediately concerned about Grant, the boy he had loved so intensely and watched over with such overinformed care. Every small illness had been a matter of professional concern. Every psychological latitude had been granted him for fear of repression or introversion. Every toy and record and book he had wanted had been given him on some occasion or other, sometimes even on the pretext of an occasion. Richard was proud of Grant. It had hurt him when Grant turned away from them so early to gaze at Lois Lehmann, to join the chorus of boys who followed her around. He found it hard to accept that his Grant—with the cheerful, independent, little-boy face, the red, unruly curls and the wide, innocent eyes—was among her captives. He saw nothing in Lois, except simpering sexual lure and a radiant body. He saw everything in Grant: Minna's good looks, his own curious and efficient mind, agile fingers and, he had thought, their love of good living.

Grant was asleep next morning when Richard left early for the hospital. Friday? Saturday morning, was it? It was raining that morning, that she was sure of. She had an appointment to have her hair cut at ten, so she left a note for Grant saying she'd be home at twelve and would make breakfast for him when she got back. Waiting in the rain for the bus at her corner of Central Park West, she saw Grant's motorcycle, its plastic cover weighed down with water, chained to the rail beside the delivery entrance to the apartment house. 'My God. All the way down the Saw Mill River Parkway on *that*?' she thought. Before noon she was back at the apartment. Grant was gone. He'd written a postscript to her note: 'Thanks for the use of the hall. Grant.' Except for that sentence there was no sign that he'd been there at all. The bed was made, he had not used the towel she had left for him in the bathroom.

Minna pulled off the highway and decided to have some coffee and something to eat. No sign that he had been there at all. Perhaps it had all been a fantasy: his coming, his story, his departure on his Harley Davidson, which, the police told them the next night, Sunday it was . . . Sunday, yes, was found completely wrecked—'totaled' was their word—beside the abutment into which he had crashed head on. His cracked helmet was returned to them, the straps inside heavily coated with blood. His wallet, containing fifty dollars; his old draft card; his driver's license and a worn, browned photo of Lois when she was sixteen years old were given to Richard after the inquest. 'Accidental death,' the certificate read. No pictures of Johnny or Lolita in the wallet, only Lois, the fatally golden girl who was his one love, the unfaithful wife of an eternally faithful lover and husband. 'Accidental death? Oh no,' she thought. 'No death was ever less accidental.'

Minna stretched her tired back and stiff legs, leaning against the car. She locked it carefully and went into the fast-food restaurant, the first place she came to after the exit from the turnpike. Over the door the sign said GOURMET FAST FOOD. She grimaced and thought she would record the lovely name in her notebook when she had had some coffee. It was five o'clock; the sun was already low. She decided she would not waste much time on this stop but push on until all the light was gone. It was Richard's belief (he always did the driving, feeling insecure, he said, with someone else at the wheel) that trips accomplished in one long push seemed shorter and less onerous. Reversing her earlier plan, she decided to test the theory. 'Keep going,' she commanded herself. At the counter she ordered a plain doughnut and coffee. The doughnut was clearly a survivor from breakfast, sturdy, solid, tough. She dipped it into the coffee and told herself, 'I've got to leave Grant behind. From the Pennsylvania Turnpike to this point, he's been in the car with me. I've got to put him out, along with the Beresford, The Rocks, everything that defines the old life I want to inter, to consign to the past.' She stirred her coffee dregs, in which swam the remnants of the doughnut. 'No further! You come along with me no further,' she said to her son. She repeated the injunction to Mrs. Grant Roman, who stood beside him looking up at her husband's red hair and gentle face. To her grandchildren, who were playing somewhere nearby, she was silent, not knowing them at all well, hardly believing in their existence. They were certainly no threat to the space in the Volkswagen. Now they had become Monhegan Island children, property of a bass player and a stony-hearted girl who could not be reached in time for Grant's funeral and did not cry when she heard of his death.

'Another cup, please,' she said to the counter girl. She was trying to prolong the time out of the car, relax from the compulsively bent driving posture. During the service for Grant, Minna had not been able to keep her mind on her dead son, who seemed absent, somehow, in both body and spirit from the chapel. She was absorbed in remembering something he had told her about funerals in South Korea. 'Pallbearers wear cotton masks over their mouths, you know, like people in cities who have difficulty breathing the bad air. Pallbearers believe the *dead* have to be protected from contagion, not the living. It's a funny sight, those funerals, six masked men bearing a coffin in which you know an unmasked dead man lies.' Should they all have been wearing masks, she wondered, to protect poor Grant from the contagion of living?

At nine Minna stopped for the night on the outskirts of Indianapolis. She parked her car at a motel, registered and walked across the street to a place that advertised, in a neon sign, ALL-NITE HAMBURGERS. Too tired to eat, she picked at the meat, setting little pieces of it on top of the pickle she had cut up. She forced down the french fries, drank two cups of black coffee and walked wearily back to the motel. At her door—number 13, she noted grimly—she patted the VW that had done so well so far but had seemed, each time she climbed reluctantly back into it, to be growing smaller and less hospitable. At the end of the drive she had been so tired that the three lanes she was traveling blended into one; she found herself driving on the berm of the road. All the distinguishing marks of Indiana she had thought she might encounter melded into one repetitive landscape: low garages, barns, diners, farmhouses glaring in the brutal sun and set back from the interstate in groves of dusty cottonwood trees, rusting implements and old cars left in corners of summer-browned rough fields.

'Indiana,' she thought. 'And across the whole state of Ohio'—turning the key in the lock and putting up the little chain. Richard used to say the whole Middle West could be summed up in one word: 'corn,' and if you wanted to be wordy, you might add 'soybeans.' 'Richard,' Minna said aloud to the mirror that hung crookedly over the Art Deco dresser, searching into it for his face. She realized he stood beside her without leaving an image in the mirror. She lay on the bed, too tired to go through the ritual of teeth, washing and undressing. She never knew whether he lay down beside her or not. She was asleep at once.

At dawn she was awake. 'No sense lying here,' she thought. She got up stiffly, washed her face, left the door of the little box of a room ajar, climbed into the VW, all in one continuous movement because she thought if she gave consideration to these activities she would not be able to perform any one of them. She had gone some miles west on Route 74 before she became aware of Richard sitting beside her, propped up against her boxes of three- by five-inch cards, on which were written, in her careful scholar's hand, her notes for the study of the lives of five factory workers—all women—who had died in the Triangle Shirtwaist Factory fire in 1911 in New York City. She realized he had been sitting there since she left Indianapolis, perhaps even since she pulled out of the Manhattan garage with a false sense of total freedom.

'Richard,' she said, looking straight ahead. 'I'm ready to tell you what I feel. I haven't been able to before, in all the years of our marriage. We never talked of such things, of anything really except things of use. We were too busy, *doing* for ourselves, for our dinners, for Grant, for our security and our futures, for those we considered our friends, and for our elderly parents. We bought our living spaces, in suburbia and on the coast, all but this last one when we holed up without responsibilities, we told each other, in the Beresford, with Central Park for our garden, the Sheep Meadow for our lawn, the Reservoir for our lake. We decorated, we furnished, we discarded and we bought: coffee makers, and blenders, radios and phonographs as big as coffins, cars that smelled of newness and proud possession. We bought clothes. God, how we bought clothes. We packaged ourselves as attractively as our homes, for our friends' admiration, and when we were finished with our clothes we gave everything, in great gestures of generosity, to Goodwill and the Salvation Army. We traveled often. But somehow I got more pleasure from making plans and plotting projected itineraries than from the places themselves when we finally arrived. Maybe we were tired from the rigorous preparations and purchases. It was always so. The Caribbean had bad food, the south of France was hot, the Cape was crowded, the water in Maine too cold, London too expensive. But in the months of anticipation, all these places had been without flaw.'

Richard made no move to reply or to contribute, made no contradictions. Minna went on, 'Well, I grant you, we did have fun. We walked, sunned, snorkeled, swam, floated and sailed pleasurably, played with our son and waited anxiously for him to learn to walk, acquire teeth and words, and then sentences. Do you remember reading to him end-lessly, talking to him about everything in careful sentence structure because we were told what echoes young children were? But he, choosing his silences carefully, talked back very little. We worried until he managed to learn to swim, to ride a bicycle: what anxiety! We loved him and he lived with us patiently, tolerantly. Even as a boy he started to love someone else. We never had a chance at the grown man.

'And our work. Well, we had that. We had parallel careers, which never touched at any point. I disliked your colleagues, you were bored with mine. Your profession was of importance to the world, mine much less. Still, we worked long hours, and when we stopped, played as hard. We listened avidly to chamber music, we read new novels and went to the opera and the ballet (walking down Columbus Avenue to City Center from the Beresford and back again) without having to be part of the taxi battle. We barbecued meat on the spit in one kitchen and before that in our Vineyard garden and made elaborate drinks in the blender. Everything we did, you cutting and suturing, I correcting and lecturing, had the same hard, driving conviction behind it. I cleaned when the maid didn't come, we cooked on her night out, we marketed, as my mother used to call it, and cooked for our friends to display our skill, and they marveled at the results. We gave them our recipes with secret pride. (Grant, of course, resisted our culinary accomplishments. He ate only foods he could cover with catsup.) We paid our debts and our charges and our taxes, and when your early-April temper grew too hot we hired someone to figure them for us. Once more childless when Grant went off to Brown, we settled into the grassless, elevated apartment, with no attic and no cellar to leak, with flower beds and herbs restricted to boxes outside the windows and a motorized lift in place of staircases, flagstone walks and mowed pathways.

155

'We passed through childbirth, moves, promotions, mumps and roseola, women's monthly plague, drink, too much of it, hiatal hernias and hemorrhoids, wandering desires, sleepless nights, periodontists and psychiatrists, laundry crises (a black sock washed with all the white shirts), athlete's foot, psoriasis and poison ivy, checks that bounced and small gains in the stock market, flus and bronchial phlegms, mosquito bites, yes, and squirrel bites, but no, that was mine and a very long time ago. Baldness afflicted you; my body hair grew sparse after menopause, my temper short; your impatience with fools, nurses and women in general grew noticeable, especially after you passed your fiftieth birthday.

'But look: we have outgrown our guilts, about our parents, about each other. About Grant: I don't know. Are we responsible? Did some lack in us force him to compensate with a mean girl? We are here, having come through depressions, the Jazz Age, the Crash, wars and the death of Grant. He is gone, a nonachiever from the very start of his life, saved from a war only to succumb to a feminine twist of the knife in the heart. I've outlived my now-famous classmate who surrendered too early, who attained fame with her poetry and by gas. I tell all the people who want to interview me about her that I never knew her well, which surely is true. I understand her better now because I've outlived her, but I had no part in her interior life, for which I feel some guilt. You've outlived your alcohol-sodden college roommate who spent part of every year at a "health farm" drying out. We've got past all the pains and breaks and illicit pleasures.'

At Danville, just over the state line into Illinois, Minna decided to have some coffee and food. The terrible, inexorable demands of Route 74 had set up a percussion behind her eyes. She began to see puddles in the center of the road. She began to wonder if some of the trucks that passed her wanted her VW off the road, whether the low farms, which seemed entirely without people, had been decimated by a bomb just before she passed them. For twenty miles she had not seen a soul on either side of the road. Her imaginings and her paranoia about the trucks grew. 'I'd better stop, for sure,' she thought, and took the next exit into Danville.

'All right, Dr. Roman,' she said to her husband without bothering to look over at him. 'We'll stop for a bit. I think I'm getting absentminded. Next thing you know, I'll drive into somebody's barn, kill a pig or something and end up in jail. I'll be fined some outlandish amount. It'll have been a prize boar he was raising for the Illinois State Fair.' She laughed foolishly, drove into the first driveway she came to and pulled up in front of a Donut Shoppe.

That night Minna stayed in Rock Island, a little more than an hour from Iowa City. She was too weary to drive farther. The place she found to stay was close to the river. After a supper of chow mein that made her feel queasy even as she ate, she found a place along the waterfront that was not blocked by parking lots or restaurants. Easing herself down on the rough, stained pier, she took off her shoes and put her feet into the water. It was green with scum, in which floated metal can tops, foam cups, straws and condoms. 'So I greet the mighty Mississippi,' she said aloud to the slowly eddying, thick water at her feet.

Next morning, feeling grateful that she was almost at the end of the terrible trek, she rose at six, had some instant coffee and a Danish pastry, what the motel called a 'Continental breakfast.' After she had turned in her key at the desk and come outside to breathe the fresh early-morning air, she noticed the sign over the entrance to the place: DE LUXE BUDGET MOTEL, it read. 'An oxymoron,' she thought. 'Well, hardly, or maybe, or perhaps both, or nothing,' she said to Richard, who had returned to the seat beside her, silent, as if he were waiting for her to continue her monologue. It seemed to her he was smoking his pipe. 'Still here, are you? Well, you picked the better place to sleep. That bed was hardly big enough for two of us to share.' When he failed to comment, she was caught up again in her conversation with him. '*Share*. A good place to start. We believed in it. Share the wealth, share the driveway, share the bed, the responsibility. We bought shares. Everything seemed so safe. Our money was safe. Our retirements, not so far away now, all safe. We have a safe-deposit box and safe investments. Safety in privacy and double locks and sometimes in numbers, in three,' she reminded Richard. 'In three we thought and then when that uncrowded number failed, when we buried our broken-up son, you said, "We'll be all right, we'll manage. Other people do. We'll make out all right." And I said, I remember saying when you held my hand and while we waited for the hired black limousine to take us home from the cemetery, "You think we'll get over this, don't you? Well, today I think neither of us will." You said, "I don't understand what you mean." And I said, under my breath, "You'll see." '

The light now sat upon the low hills and draws of the Iowa landscape, beautiful because the cornfields, in various states of growth, made abstract patterns on the gentle rises. The odors from the fields were wet and heavy, vetivernal and lush. The Bug moved more heavily than at the start of its journey, as though it were tired of its burdens and people. To the man sitting jammed between cardboard boxes Minna said, 'It's unusual for me to talk like this. For you to listen so patiently is unusual too. We may have survived, as you said that day, but we failed. We failed slowly, not all at once. Our marriage suffered a sluggish, torpid disintegration. Love went first, it always does—isn't that true? How could it possibly endure for almost four decades? Custom, service, duty, ritual set in, and worst of all, irrational disappointment that the bright light had gone out. We each blamed the other. Next to go was that terrible sidekick of love, jealously. No longer did it plague—or enliven—our passion. Did this happen to us both at once? I cannot remember. My friend Liz used to claim that nothing comes out even, nothing in this life, and she was right, of course. What happened next? Concern, that was it. I grew concerned about everything, like my mother used to be. Except for one thing: when you were sick I felt an odd sort of relief. You were mortal. Someday, I thought, I may be free. I know I didn't want you to die. I loved you in my way, in my loss-flooded way, but I wanted to be free. When *I* was sick, you seemed concerned, but, I thought, not deeply. You saw such bad pain where you worked that mine seemed to you exaggerated. Our mutual and constant concern was for Grant. Every one of his illnesses seemed at first to be life-threatening. We always felt we might lose him, we ached at the thought. You saw all possible complications, I saw only one, the possibility he might die. The bond between us weakened under the pressures of my love for him. I tried to hold it in check. But I must have revealed it to you with my concern for his every move and fever and cough. (Didn't we all read too much Freud, and then fear for the objects of our love?) Mine was true love for that lovely redheaded boy, his blue eyes full of questions and early despair. It came hand in hand with my passionate dislike of his silly, pretty-faced girl-love.'

Richard may have nodded, she thought, but she could not turn her head away from the road to find out. She felt herself growing empty. She thought she might as well go on until there was nothing more left to say. 'We have, I admit, had one very good thing. We had all the varied and curious and satisfying pleasures of sex. Almost nightly, all those years, because you brought your medical school instruction to bear on the subject and taught me to believe that long intervals between sexual acts depleted the source, that the more often we "did it," as you said, the greater would be our pleasure, and the longer our desire would last. It was true. You were right. It did get better, it did last. We accepted no excuses from each other, even the imminence of Grant's birth, even a short time after his birth. We were at it regularly, it served as our Sominex and our muscle relaxant. After it, I always slept well. Intercourse was the one bond that did not wither: we kept our marriage alive in the pleasures of its variety. I was a wonder to myself and to my friends, who had to listen to my boasting. After menopause, which came, I thought, rather late to me—was I fifty-four, or fifty-five? It was long use of the pill, they said—we went on practicing our private craft with new delight, it seemed to me. You never questioned the success of our marriage. Sex for you was the keystone and core; if it was there and was good, everything held. Now at sixty, during this blessed, long semester's "leave without pay," as my college calls it, and after, when it is clear that I have left you (for that is what I am planning to do when this academic stint is over), what I will miss most will be our enduring sexual accomplishments, our mutual enjoyment during four decades of gratification. I suppose that, more than anything, it was a source of pride. I *am* proud. . . .'

NEXT TWO EXITS U. OF IOWA. 'Which one? Well, I suppose it doesn't matter. I'll take the first and see where that gets me.' Minna looked at the map of the city sent to her by the chairman of the department, and figured out a route into the city and to the place called Iowa House in which a room had been rented for her. After some wrong turns and rerouting because the map did not show one-way streets and even this small town seemed to have a plethora of them, she parked in front of the brick building that sat stolidly on the bank of a river. 'I've made it. I'm here. This begins a new term, the short term, the term of my change into a single person. I'm on my own.'

Minna turned to her silent rider and said, 'This is where you get off, friend-husband. No further. Have you listened to my long tirade? Do you know what I am trying to tell you? Probably not. I'm not sure I am clear about it all myself.' She took two suitcases from the VW. When she looked for Richard, he was gone. She thought she could still smell the tang of his pipe tobacco.

The room the department chairman had reserved for her in Iowa House, a campus hotel for visitors, was pleasant, cool, very clean and somewhat monastic, especially after the steam-heated overfurnishing of her New York apartment. Two large uncurtained windows looked out to grass and the narrow Iowa River. The bathroom was large and very white, the closet so cool that Minna stored her half-gallon of Beef-eater on the floor and needed no ice when it came time for her drink before dinner. She pulled the leatherette chair to the window, put her papers, books and portable Royal type-writer on the large round table beside it. Her clothes and shoes filled half the closet; her luggage and packing cases were piled in the other half. Over the double bed, covered with a chaste white chenille spread, there was a good light; a solid-looking black telephone stood on the stand beside it. There was a low, ample clothes chest, and a long mirror above it. The walls were white and bare of hotel art. The door locked with a key and a chain. Furnished in this way, the room felt spare, almost careful, about itself and its single occupant.

Minna took her dinner at restaurants in town, and then walked back in the dusk to her room. Sometimes she was too tired to make the trip up and then down the hill to the center of town, so she had supper in the cafeteria downstairs in Iowa House. She found this restful. The room was filled with students and junior faculty, not one of whom knew her. She sat near a window, watching the river ducks come home to their nests under the trees for the night. She thought of her extraordinary freedom from domestic chores and human relationships. With the morning's copy of *The Daily Iowan* propped up beside her cup of coffee, she surrendered to long periods of solitary pleasure, congratulating herself on having achieved such eremetic quiet, this sense of reclusiveness. For the first time in her long life she was entirely alone, living alone, eating alone. She was astonished to find she was not in the least lonely.

In her office mailbox when she first arrived was an invitation from someone in the department of English, asking her to talk to a class in contemporary poetry. 'You are welcome to come to any class that is convenient for you. We meet Mondays and Thursdays at one. The students are reading *Poems Returned from Saint Elizabeth's* now. Anything you could tell them about Maud Noon would be most welcome. Perhaps you may know that I did my doctoral thesis on Noon, so of course *I* shall be delighted. . . .'

The assistant professor, a thin, energetic, loquacious woman named Janice Sinatra ('Before you ask, let me assure you, I'm *no* relation') hustled her into the classroom and sat beside her behind a table. She began an elaborate introduction, in which Minna's academic past was quickly reduced to her college and her title. A long peroration followed. Minna appeared in it as the friend and confidante of the celebrated American poet who died tragically so young. The introduction took a long time and was designed to demonstrate

Professor Sinatra's knowledge of Maud's life and work. 'Tell us first, Dr. Roman, how you came to know Noon.' 'We had rooms next to each other in Hewitt, at Barnard College.' Minna hesitated, looking at a redheaded blue-eyed child in a T-shirt that read HARVARD. 'It was, um, in 1939.' 'Tell us what she was like then,' said Professor Sinatra. 'Well, first let me say that although we lived close together, I never got to know her as well as . . . as I might have. She studied hard, and went out very little. I was closer to the photographer Liz Becker, who lived on the other side of Maud in our senior year—' Professor Sinatra broke in to say to the class, 'Elizabeth Becker, you remember, took that wonderful picture of Otto Mile when he was dying in a mental hospital. It was she—I'm right, am I not, Dr. Roman?— who rescued the poems that form the body of this book we're now studying.' 'Yes,' said Minna. There was a long silence brought about by the curtness of Minna's response. Then a boy in the back of the room said, 'Did she think about death a lot, the way she does in all these poems?' Minna said, 'No. I don't think so. I never heard her talk about death. But I knew her years before she . . . died, and saw her very little after we graduated. I went away to graduate school, she stayed in New York and went to Columbia. We married, but you know, different sorts of men who did different sorts of things. So we only met a few times, when Elizabeth Becker instigated a sort of reunion now and then.' 'What was she like when you all got together?' asked Professor Sinatra, seeming avid for anything that Minna might say. 'The same. The same as she had been in college. Quiet and rather secretive about herself, but always very interested in what everyone else was doing. She asked a lot of questions about my area of research, she always wanted to know everything about what shows Liz was having, in what magazines she was publishing her photographs. The last time I saw her, was, I think after the children had gone to live with her mother. We had lunch together up near Columbia. She seemed sad. I asked to read some of her poems and she gave me a large sheaf of carbon copies of them and said not to bother returning them. I took them home and read them and thought them quite wonderful. After she . . . was dead I realized she had burned a lot of her work and that I had the only copies of some things.' 'So you are responsible for having them published, like Max Brod with Franz Kafka's work, and Robert Bridges for Gerard Manley Hopkins?' 'No, nothing so elevated as all that. I knew a man in publishing, Jay Laughlin, who was a patient of my husband's. He came to dinner one night, and I showed them to him. That's the only part I had in it all.' A girl sitting at the side of the room said, 'Did you like her? As a person, I mean.' Minna hesitated. Poor Maud, she thought, did I like her, her with her vast, unattractive person and self-absorbed brilliant self? 'Yes, I think I liked her. Why do you ask?' The girl twisted her long hair in one hand and looked embarrassed. 'Because, well, she seems, from all the biographies, a person it would be hard to like. Now that she's dead, and the way she died, well, it might be easier to like her now.' The class laughed. Professor Sinatra looked stern and disapproving of the note of levity in the question. Minna said, 'She is, was and is, a very good poet. But I didn't know it then. Now I do. And the older I get, the more I think about her, the more present and real she seems to me, more than she was when we lived next door to each other in Hewitt Hall. That,' she added lamely, 'says something about the force of art.'

The class proceeded to look at the poems in the books they all had before them. Minna listened to their weak interpretations and to Professor Sinatra's confident, sharp corrections and comments. When she was appealed to, Minna said only, 'I'm a historian. I know very little about poetry.'

Then she laughed. 'But I know what I like, and I like Maud's stuff.' The class applauded her sophomoric response, and stood up to leave. 'Thank you very much, Dr. Roman,' said Professor Sinatra. She sounded disappointed. 'That was . . . illuminating.' Minna nodded, clutched the paperback copy of Maud's poems that had been presented to her, and vowed silently that never, never again in her life would she say anything in public—or private, for that matter—about poor famous Maud Noon.

A few congenial members of the history department separated themselves from the others and left the late October faculty meeting together. The department had made its way through the first half of the agenda, and everyone was thirsty, hungry, disgruntled and uncomfortable on the camp chairs they had been occupying since three o'clock. The chairman declared an adjournment for dinner. Minna started to walk over to the Universal Joint ('The *what?*' she had asked Rob Altmann, when the vote was taken among the friends for an acceptable eating place, the single unanimous vote of the afternoon). As they left Schaeffer Hall, she chose Rob Altmann to walk beside. He was a tall, bearded fellow who wore a cossack blouse buttoned at the neck and at the ends of the wide sleeves. He taught Russian history. His eyes were blue-black and set far back into his head under bushy black eyebrows. Habitually, he tucked worsted peasant's pants into his high black suede boots. A curly black cuff of hair remained on his head. Otherwise he was bald and covered his bare head with a visored workman's cap. Minna told him when they met he resembled a youthful Tolstoy. Rob approved of her comparison, approved even more of her attention to his clothing.

'That was one dull gathering,' Rob said to Minna, holding her elbow with a show of gallantry as they crossed Washington Street. 'There wasn't one single topic I had any interest in whatsoever.' Minna nodded. Her boredom had been so great she now felt the need to dwell on some subject far from curriculum reform, scheduling, adjunct hiring, some restorative topic. She asked Rob about his summer visit to southern Siberia she had heard mentioned by a woman in her research group. Minna said to Rob, 'Why there?' and then smiled. 'Second time I've questioned a destination in the last half hour.'   'Yes. Well, I went because I'm interested in schism in old Russia, small groups of people who broke away from the state religion, particularly the Old Believers. They resisted the changes in the Russian Orthodox ritual in the seventeenth century and left not only the church but also the region. Seems the Patriarch Nikon "renewed" the liturgy and changed the prayer book. So the Old Believers, perhaps three or four hundred persons, broke away from the church.'   'Interesting, isn't it? That's what happened in recent years to the reformed Catholic Church, isn't it?'   'Oh yes. But the fascinating thing about the Old Believers is the extent to which they went to preserve their faith. Peter the Great decided he would tax the schismatics. . . .' At the entrance to the Universal Joint, Rob pulled the wooden door toward them and pushed Minna gently into the dark restaurant. The others followed as Rob held the door for them. 'And, rather amazing for that time, declared that his regime henceforth would be entirely secular. So the Old Believers were probably the first group to rebel against Czarist rule, though of course not for political reasons.'

The six historians who had cut away from the department to have supper together took a large round table in a corner. Minna was the only woman ('probably because I am only a visiting professor,' she thought). She said hello to Allan Olcott, on her left. He wore a Yale tie, a stiffly starched shirt and a beautifully tailored suit. Then she made a point of smiling and nodding across the table to Bill Oleson, about to retire, she'd heard; to Leonard Reiss, the celebrated Civil War expert; and to Jamie Mirston, who, she thought she remembered from the introduction when first she arrived, was 'in' English history. The women in her pioneer-history group must have gone off together to another restaurant, probably because they hadn't been invited here. The women were instructors and assistant professors, so naturally (Minna smiled to herself at her use of the word) they were excluded from this elevated circle of friends. She could hear Rob Altmann's loud voice coming from her right and realized that her conversation with him, under the influence of the round table perhaps, had become a lecture. 'Vasily Peskov, a friend of mine in Moscow who is a journalist, had read about one family of Old Believers who still survived. He wanted to interview them. So we drove to within a day of where he had heard they were and then walked the rest of the way into wilderness and by luck came upon two old huts built against a hillside.'   'What do you all want to drink?' asked a tall blond waiter, clearly a student, who wore a white apron wound around him at the waist and reaching below his knees.   'I'll have an ale, and nachos right away. I hate to drink without eating,' said Leonard Reiss to the waiter.   'For me too,' called Rob. The waiter wrote rapidly on a green pad.   'What's the soup?' asked Bill Oleson, winking at the waiter, indicating, Minna thought, that he was an habitué who knew there was always 'the soup.'   'The usual, cream-something-or-other. I'm not quite sure what,' said the waiter and smiled an enchanting little-boy smile at Oleson, whom he seemed to know. Minna, watching the waiter, turned pale. She had seen a smile like that before, on Grant in his adolescence, when he was still trying to please her, before the name Lois began to appear in every sentence. The others decided they would settle for tacos or cheeseburgers. Minna had trouble deciding. Her composure had been shaken. She felt suddenly sunk into the past, captivated by the present, unhungry. She disliked Mexican food, clearly the Universal Joint's specialty, and distrusted the meat in burgers. The blond waiter came around the table and stood behind her. 'What'll you have, ma'am?' Against her will she turned around in her chair to look at him. 'The soup?' he asked. His voice was soft and high. Surprised, Minna stared at him. He looked down at her, waiting patiently for her order. His nose was thin and long, his lips were unexpectedly red for a boy (A boy, is he, or a man? Minna wondered). His cheeks were rough-red and looked as if they had never been shaved. 'An Iowa farm boy,' Minna thought. 'I'll bet.' She went on looking at him, unable to think of anything she wanted to eat, unable to think of anything but how beautiful, how much like her poor son. 'A beer?' he said, trying to be helpful, but getting tired of standing there, Minna thought. 'We have Bud on draft.'   'No, no, thank you, no beer. I'll have the soup. Whatever kind it is.'   He laughed. 'You'll take your chances?' he said and flashed again his wondrous smile. At the corners of his mouth, small virgules appeared. Further back in his cheeks were two deep, disarming dimples. 'Want anything with that?'   'Coffee,' she managed to say, engrossed as she was in his beautiful face. 'That'll be fine.'   'Soup and coffee?' he asked, continuing to smile at the absurdity of the order. Minna looked at him hard, and nodded.

'He was in his nineties, I guess, this bedraggled fellow that came out of the hut. He said his name was Karl Osipovich Lykov and that he lived there with his two sons and two daughters. His wife had been dead ten years. In the next two days we learned that his family had been out of touch with the rest of the world for almost sixty years. They left their first hideout after the Revolution because of the Reds' views on religion. Things were getting worse for them in 1919, so Lykov took his family and a few other Old Believers and moved on to the rugged, unpopulated hills near the headwaters of the Abakan River—' 'Where would that be, in relation to Moscow, for example?' asked Bill Irwin, trying, Minna thought, to break into the monologue. 'In the Sayan Mountains in southern Siberia. At least two hundred miles from any other human settlement in any direction. His sons and daughters, now in their late forties, had never seen another person until we arrived. One daughter cried every time she looked at me. She kept saying, "It is the curse of the devil. It has arrived," or some such thing, Peskov said. They were all terrified to have been found. One son said we must be the Kaiser's soldiers in disguise.'

The waiter put nachos and ale in front of Rob, temporarily blocking Rob's narrative while he inspected the dish and the drink. Then he started again. 'But the amazing thing was, they all survived, all but the wife, living in a soot-filled blackened log hut for sixty years. They used no matches or soap. Washing was apparently anathema, so their clothes and their bodies were never washed, and man, I tell you, they *stank*. That hut was smelly and filthy. But there was no question of our contact with them. They thought we were carrying infections, bodily and spiritual ones, I guess, so they would not touch us, even to shake hands. God, they were foul, and yet . . .' The waiter finished distributing the plates and steins and bottles at the right places without asking any questions. As he came around to Minna she thought, 'God, I hope he doesn't smile at me like that again.' 'They live on onions, potatoes, turnips and the fish the sons catch and rabbits and birds they trap. And yet . . .' 'Very good, this stuff,' said Jamie Mirston to Allan Olcott. 'Just enough food for us prisoners who have to get back to the institution by seven.' 'Yes, indeed, quite good,' said Allan, but not loud enough to stop Rob's discourse.   'It's their absolute faith, their pure belief, amid all that isolation and stench. The two nights we stayed they prayed together every few hours all through the night. We could hear them in there from the sleeping bags we had put down near their cooking fire. And then, at any moment during the day—we could never figure out what brought it on—they would stop what they were doing, fall on their knees and were absolutely still, praying, calling aloud to God, or listening to the old man read from the Scriptures.'   'This beer is all right,' said Leonard to Allan.   'Anyone listening to all of this?' Rob said.   'All of us,' said Irwin, 'with what is called bated breath.'   'We want to know how it all comes out,' said Allan.   'Especially how it ends,' said Leonard. Rob laughed with everyone, and began to drink his ale, which was now flat and warm. For a while there could be heard the sound of tacos breaking against their teeth, the restrained slurp of soup, and the laughter of students at the bar and townspeople at nearby tables.   'They must have had a very strong family bond,' said Minna in a low voice to Rob, feeling sorry about the way everyone had turned off the Russian historian.   'That's the strange thing. Dmitri, one of the sons, was sick. They had moved him out of the hut. He lay some distance from the hut, under a tree, covered with sacking, the same kind of material everyone in the family wore for pants and shirts and skirts. Peskov examined him and thought he must be suffering from some sort of stomach trouble. We asked the old man about him, but he would say nothing. No member of the family ever came near him or brought him food that we could see. Peskov thought they were afraid of catching whatever he had, so they would not touch him. The daughter, the one who cried all the time, said once of Dmitri, "It is of the devil," so it may be they thought that to touch him was to catch his evil.'   'How odd,' said Minna. The others sat still, thinking about the lessons of the Old Believers' lives. 'And terrible,' she added.

'Terrible,' said Rob. 'We decided that anything that got in the way of their prayer life, their incessant reading of the Scriptures, was evil. When Peskov told the old man there had been another world war since they left civilization, he got very angry and said it was all Peter the Great's fault, him and his cursed plotting with Germans. All evil was centered in Peter, he was the devil, along with Nikon.'   'How much do we leave for a tip?' Leonard, to whom the waiter had presented the check, asked of the table at large.   'Multiply the total by fifteen percent and divide by six,' said Minna.   'Fine,' said Leonard. 'You do all that,' and passed the check to her. After a good deal of change making, addition and subtraction, the matter was settled. Minna waited for the waiter to come to her place and pick up the motley collection of bills and coins. She handed him the money. He smiled and thanked her. She found herself having trouble standing up, but she managed by looking away from the waiter and starting precipitately for the door. 'You left your purse,' said the waiter, behind her.   'Oh my,' she said. 'How stupid. Thank you.'   'Not at all,' he said, and smiled. Minna, believing she was going to suffocate, reached for the door and pushed it open. On the street, the little group of historians was waiting. 'Ready?' they asked her.   'Yes.' Rob, Allan and Minna walked together toward Schaeffer Hall. 'Did you find yourself liking the family? As people?' she asked.   'I suppose so, although I could not stand being near them, they stank so. At the end of our days there, Peskov asked them if they would like him to look into the possibility of their resettling. At that suggestion, the whole family stared at us. The son and daughters said nothing. Their father pushed them hastily into the hut. They refused to come out again or maybe it was that the father would not let them come out. We could hear him in there praying. We took our packs and started out of the little clearing, walking, it seemed forever, until we came upon our car. But you asked me if I liked them. Well, I admired their devotion, their perfect obedience to what they believed was the will of God.' 'Are you planning to write about them?' 'Some day. Meanwhile in the middle of a futile meeting like the one this afternoon, with all those little academic egos fighting for *Lebensraum* and recognition, I like to remember Lykov. His simplicity. His otherworldliness. His extraordinary piety.'

Once again as they recrossed Washington Street, Rob held her elbow. It made Minna feel her sixty years, something she had forgotten about when she looked at the shining face of the blond waiter. Feeling odd, she shook off the thought of him and asked, 'What happened to the son who was sick?' 'He was dying when we left. I suppose he's dead by now.' Minna frowned. 'When you think about them and their virtues in the middle of tonight's meeting, remember that most human beings are selfish. And cruel. Leaving a son exposed to die, for whatever reason. Lord!' Rob agreed. At Schaeffer Hall they joined the rest of the diners. Together, they climbed the stairs to the meeting room.

November 12, 1978. 'Dear Liz: You ask about Iowa City. Well, I may be seeing it in a rather roseate way, for reasons I will tell you about, but in your query I detect a tone of true urban doubt. Answer: it's astonishingly pleasant, a humane city with no traffic or pollution, no hassle, no crowds. Its streets are wide, its buildings low except for a few medical and hospital buildings. There are many small pleasant stores manned (and womaned) by polite and handsome students. Despite the widespread, entirely uninformed beliefs of my city friends (you among them, old girl) that everything here is flat, dull, uninteresting, uncivilized, there are, for one thing, hills so steep in the city itself that it is a trial sometimes to climb them. The autumn landscape (now inching into winter) outside the confines of the city is lovely. Rolling hills, dark draws, little farm ponds, hay piled in bales at the borders of fields that are gray, brown or dark yellow with the remains of cornstalks, a few still green with late-planted barley. There is no high drama in the land out there, but wonderful variety, subtle differences in line and color configuration. It is a gentle city, a delicate countryside. Outside the city are small communities of Amish, Mennonite and Amana people. And over it all, a sky so enormous that it seems to sit over the whole southern part of the state like a blue watch cap pulled down over the ears of a giant. The sky, and what it covers, is customarily even-tempered, unassertive and benign.

'If I sound somewhat rhapsodic it may be the pleasure I have found in the landscape. But there is something else, a phenomenon I am about to confide in you because of your affection for human curiosities. You will recognize my freakishness. I will write it bluntly: *I am in love.* You may gasp, laugh, shudder, snicker. You will say, "Ridiculous, absurd, nonsense, *you*, a sixty-year-old woman, a mother once, a grandmother, for God's sake." I too am aghast. Leaving New York at the end of August (I apologize for not having called to say good-bye), I was intent to reduce a lifetime of possessions to the barest essentials, more particularly, to what would fit into the VW. I was whittled down to a Giacometti-like thinness. It was a curious shuffling-off process, putting behind me (or into the trash) possessions, events, and persons, not just storing them, but eliminating them, returning them to the forgotten and abandoned past. Grant's death. My long marriage. My job, all the detritus of six decades of living. I felt weak and frightened, as if I had been through a purgation. By the time I arrived in

Iowa City, the molting process was over. I settled down to work, to the course I teach, "Woman and Labor in the Nineteenth Century," and to the research project on midwestern pioneer women that I told you about, I think.

'For the first seven weeks I felt wonderful, even resurrected, if that is the right word. Perhaps rejuvenated would be better. I was healthy, energetic and yes, *young*. I could not believe it. Three weeks ago I waited at a light behind a car on whose bumper sticker was the old cliché "Today is the the first day of the rest of your life." I laughed. But do you know, I have felt this way here, almost every day and even more so now. I believe it. I know it is true, that this unsuitable and unnatural youth I am feeling is accompanied by an even stronger, stranger feeling of moving backward in time instead of the old weary sense of moving inexorably ahead. One example of all this fantasy: since I broke my left ankle five years ago and then sprained it again and again, I have been increasingly frightened of stairs. I take them carefully, measuring the risers, the treads, as the old do. I look down as I descend. There are wary signs of my age in every step, I'm sure. I am decorous, I am fearful, it can be seen, I see it. Well, one evening, going down the two flights of stairs in the building in which I work, I was behind a girl who cut impatiently in front of me, as if to let me know of her irritation at my slowness. I was feeling the usual pull at the back of my legs, in the bones of my left foot. The girl looked fourteen, a long, dark ponytail, and a nose turned up, more expression than physiognomy. But of course she was older than fourteen. Somehow, I could not understand how, she went down. She never once bent her head to look down at her feet. Her feet seemed to move without the rest of her. I thought she ignored the handrail. She was so fast I could not see where her feet touched, if indeed they touched at all. Three? four? steps at a time.

Without looking. Without holding on, without being fearful. Could I do it? Well, Liz, that is exactly what I believe I did. True. It is true. I flew down, I was on the first floor before I knew what I was doing, or how I had done it. I was no longer full of the cautions of age, the slow infirmities of broken ankle and fears. I was no longer going down through time, but falling through space.

'What has all this to do with being in love? I shall tell you. It came about this way. My VW was still running, but fitfully. Some mornings it would not start and when finally it did, its transmission (I *believe* it was its transmission) noises were terrible. Two weeks ago, my fine, gallant, faithful Bug died, stopped dead in front of a drugstore on Davenport Street, and never stirred again. I stood in the street looking forlornly, I suspect, at the inert engine, when this young man stopped beside me in a white jalopy. Isn't that what we used to call those broken-down old cars in college? He wanted to know if I needed help. I knew him— it's a small town. He was the boy who had waited on my table at a local beer hall. He offered me a ride home to Iowa House; I accepted. I offered him a drink in my room; he accepted. He wanted beer. I had none but offered what I drink when alone, a small gin with ice in it from the hall ice machine. He said yes. I drank mine slowly, he swallowed the whole drink in one gulp. And asked for another. We sat in silence. Liz: I had nothing to say to the young man, the boy, as it turned out. He is twenty-two, he told me, he comes from near Dubuque, where his father has a farm. Soybean, corn, pigs, on a "section," he told me. He is tall, and very slim, he smiles like some unregenerate angel, like the small-boy Grant once did. He is very blond, so light his eyebrows and lashes seem white. He would have another, he said—he had found he liked gin as much as beer. He talked on and on about his family, his job as a waiter, his courses in agronomy out at the campus across the river. I listened, and looked at him, and sank deeper into the boy's charm.

'After he left I sat there and could not move from the chair to lock the door behind him and go to bed. I watched the moon on the Iowa River, a white disc in an enormous black bowl of sky and wondered what I was, what I had become. A foolish old woman? Lonely? A woman who had mistaken herself in her folly, who thought she had long ago spent all her passion? Or a maternal simpleton wanting a resurrected son? God, Liz, I don't know. I only know I think of nothing but that blond boy/man. The next day was the one I flew down a flight of stairs. But I ramble on. Write when you can and give Helene my regards. Is she completely recovered from the mastectomy? Yours, always, Minna.'

In her long letter, Minna enclosed a sepia photograph on a postcard. She had bought it from a rack in the drugstore. She wrote a postscript to her letter: 'Did you know about this giantess who lived in Paris in 1875? The photographer is not identified, but look at those wonderful ordinary-sized men and woman surrounding her. It reminded me of our giant, your giant, I should say. I like the tallest man in his Edwardian beard and suit, with his eyes fixed, straight across, at her bosom, and the woman who stares ahead at her waist, and the other two men with upward glances to her head, the way the mother of Aaron looked at him. My geometry tells me that if the three men are all about average, five ten or so, and come to below her shoulder, then her majestic hat with its elegant ostrich feather must reach more than seven feet into the air. The hooped skirt and brocaded jacket, her sloping shoulders, great hands and pleasant but very ordinary face: I love them all. I wish you had been there to photograph her. What do you think? Am I becoming a perverted collector of oversize persons and underage boys? Did I tell you anywhere in that welter of words the name of the boy? Lowell. Lowell Oleson. He's related, it turns out, to a man in the history department who's about to retire. Well, I'll be blunt: he's his grandson. Yours, again, Minna'

After the first evening of drinks in her room in Iowa House, Minna saw nothing of Lowell Oleson for a week. She took her new car on two trial runs to get used to automatic transmission, the unaccustomed placement of the turn signals and indicator lights, the buttons that did this or that. As she drove the empty streets of Iowa City she realized she was looking for Lowell's jalopy. She avoided contact with Bill Oleson, even stayed away from the floor his office was on. Yet one day she found herself standing beside him on the cafeteria line in the Union. 'How're you making out?' he said.   'Fine, just fine.'   'Like Iowa City?' he asked, the usual question-statement of the native to the eastern visitor.   'I do. Very much. It's a lovely town.'   'City,' he said loftily. 'It's a city.'   'Yes, of course. I apologize. So it is.'   Minna blushed because she had been caught in the expected demeaning gaffe of the New Yorker, and because Bill Oleson was her love's grandfather.

Lowell called Minna late one evening. Like a fool, a girlish old fool, she realized that she was blushing as she answered the phone. She was in her nightgown and robe, and had been doing last Sunday's *Times* crossword puzzle. She felt the heat in her face. He said, 'Hi.'   'Hello. How are you?'   'Good. And yourself?' She smiled at the form of his question, and waited. 'Can I come by for more of that clear stuff?' Her heart raced so irregularly she had to sit down on the bed. 'Yes, of course. Come along.' While she waited, she wondered if she ought to dress. Of course, *of course*. She should put all her clothes back on, girdle, stockings, bra, slip, blouse, suit, shoes, the complete uniform of proper dress. 'My God, I ought to wear my long boots and beaver coat, a hat with a veil, gloves, a muff and a lap robe.'

She had turned out all the lights but the one near the door and was in the chair watching the river when he knocked. He had stopped at the grocery store, which was just closing, and bought three bottles of cold beer. When Minna opened the door, Lowell thrust the bag at her. 'For you, ah, well, really for me,' he said. He breathed in as though he had caught the thick, sweet, heavy odor of her perfume. He breathed deeper, as though, it seemed to Minna, he felt an edge of sharpness cutting into him. She put the package down on the little table between the two chairs at the window. 'Have a seat,' she said. She brought the gin from the closet. The bottle was ice-cold. The closet lay against an outside wall of Iowa House and it was a cold night. 'I saw you tonight in the parking lot,' he said, 'going into Schaeffer.' 'Did you?' 'Can't miss that mop of blond hair when the wind is blowing through it,' he said, staring down at his sneakers. Then he looked at her, and smiled at his own gallantry. He twisted hard at the bottle top. Minna stared at him, at his choice of adjective for her hair. 'I have no extra glasses,' she said, 'except a toothbrush glass.' 'No matter. I like to drink it this way.' He took a long pull from the bottle and then put it down beside Minna's glass of gin. 'Then you must have seen my new car,' she said. 'No. What new car? When did you buy it?' 'A few days ago. The VW could not be resuscitated, for any amount of money. I had to have it put out of its misery.' Lowell laughed. 'Too bad. Did you like that little car?' 'Not especially. But it did get me here faithfully.' 'What kind did you get?' 'A Chevrolet,' and then she added—reluctantly, because ever since her impulsive and inexplicable purchase, she had not been able to explain to herself why she bought it—'a convertible.'

'Wow!' Lowell said, his thin, charming face lit with pleasure. 'Terrific. A convertible. That *is* something. Boy, I've always wanted one of those.' Minna raised her arms and pulled her fingers through her hair. Her robe fell back for a moment. She recovered herself and lowered her arms, because he was staring at her breast and the flesh of her underarms. 'Jeez,' he said. What was he thinking, that I am much older than he? No matter.

Minna described the new car, which, she told him, she had named Maud. 'Why Maud?' 'Well, it's black and there are those Tennyson lines "Come into the garden, Maud,/ For the black bat, night, has flown." I associate black with Maud. Foolish, isn't it? Then too, I once had a friend named Maud. I don't know that that's any sort of reason, either. I always name my cars.' Minna laughed. Lowell leaned forward toward her, his elbows on his knees, his face in his hands. To him she looked soft and lovely, half undressed like that, in her robe and slippers, her loose, heavy blond hair curled to her shoulders. She made him think of those flowers his mother always grew, large and sort of blowsy, especially when they were almost finished. What were they called? He could not remember.

'If you like, you can take it for a run tomorrow evening. I've got a dinner date, but after that . . . ' Her voice was low and husky and seemed to fall away at the end. She felt incapable of making a more definite arrangement. When he got up to leave, thinking the professor, as he thought of her still, wanted him to go, she put her hand on his arm.

He thought she was making fun of him, in her gentle way, when she said, holding his arm, 'I'll introduce you to Maud tomorrow night. You'll prefer her. She's very young, only nineteen miles on her at the moment.' He reddened and said, 'Don't say that. You're not old. Golly, Professor Roman, you're damned beautiful.' He slammed the door behind him, and raced to catch the elevator about to go down. Walking up the Market Street Hill toward the ratty apartment he shared with two graduate students, he suddenly remembered the name of the flowers she reminded him of: peonies. In her room, Minna still sat in her chair, watching the moonlight on the windows of the hospital buildings. She thought, 'I may well be going mad. What am I thinking about? Oh, I know very well what I am thinking about. How can this be? How can I love this inarticulate, lanky, towheaded boy? Did he say "Golly"? I have not heard "Golly" in twenty-five years.'

Lowell fell into the habit of coming to see Minna late every evening after he finished work in the Universal Joint. Sometimes she was not in when he rang her bell. He would go back down to the lobby, sit on the floor with his back to the windows and watch the elevators until she came home. She fell into the habit of looking around the lobby when she returned from a meeting, a lecture, a dinner party. They looked at each other, she nodded to him, he scrambled to his feet, dumped the *Des Moines Register* he usually read into the trash can and followed her upstairs in the next elevator. She left the door ajar. He waited and then walked slowly down the hall toward her room. She had never advised him of this caution, but he sensed she was not comfortable being seen with him. She refused to meet him for lunch at Pete's, where he usually had a sandwich and a beer with his roommates, or to allow him to accompany her, on his night off, to a student seminar on Iowa history he had said he would be interested in hearing. He well knew why he did not share her discretion. He was proud of her friendship, pleased she paid attention to him. He wanted to be able to display his connection to her in public.

Her secretiveness remained in force on the night of the seminar. She said no to his repeated requests to go with her. He was waiting in his usual place; they had their usual drinks at the window, safe because it looked out at the anonymous river. She told him about a paper she had heard that evening, about the end of the world and a group of Gypsies in Iowa in 1910.

'It was late spring, in a cool May, I think, of that year, the time of the expected appearance of Halley's Comet. On the outskirts of Fort Dodge on a high hill, hundreds of Gypsies were gathered. For months word had spread from one Gypsy family to the next, even beyond the midwestern states, with instructions that they should travel to that hill in Iowa because on that day the world would come to an end. It would be brought about by the passage of the earth through the gases of the comet. The families arrived in their wagons, which were bare. They had rid themselves of almost all their possessions and had stopped eating the day before. The wagons, brightly colored the way Gypsies decorate them, were pulled into circles, in the middle of which they lit fires for warmth. The horses were tied to the rear wheels of wagons, small children slept in the wagons, and the older ones huddled with the adults, cold, fearful, silent, hungry. All night they waited. The comet appeared, a streak of yellow light in the black sky, and then disappeared. Still they waited. By noon they were famished. They realized that nothing was going to happen to the earth, or to them. They relit the campfires, got out the few battered pots that remained to them and cooked a late, silent, sparse lunch. Then they harnessed their horses, and saying nothing to one another about their grim expectations, they drove off in every direction.'

'Jeepers, what an eerie story. Did the Gypsies ever ask who started the scare?'   'I don't know. The writer of the paper was interested in the phenomenon of belief in the end of the world, so he had a number of other examples. Only this one occurred in Iowa.'   Minna smiled at Lowell and said, 'It was an interesting paper.'   Emboldened to say something about himself, which he rarely could bring himself to do, Lowell said, 'I suppose I always think something important to me, something I do, is catastrophic, that it means the end of the world, in a way. But as time goes by, I guess you discover it rarely is.' He said nothing for a long time. Then he said, 'I want more than anything to make love to you. Would you . . . consider it?'

At two in the morning, after Lowell had left, Minna lay still and nude under the blankets. She was afraid to move, afraid to dissipate the warm flush of pleasure that remained behind her closed eyes, in her thighs, in the flesh at the back of her arms and legs. The weight of Lowell's wiry, eager boy's body on her newly young breasts was still there; her stomach was flattened by his ethereal presence, by her sudden conviction while they were making love that they were contemporaries. She was still in the dark, having turned out the light when Lowell got into bed with her so he would not be aware of her blanched triangle of scant pubic hair and the signs of age at her neck, the loosened flesh in her hips and breasts. In the darkness, in the blank isolation of the wide bed, his hands taking the place of sight, he had sprung to life at once. Enlivened by the pressure of his young presence, she greeted his entry with moisture long absent from the unused region of her sex. His clear delight at the prospect, his wild and boyish expectations aroused, she imagined, by her lush, warm flesh in his hands brought their first encounter off quickly, too quickly for Minna's slower responses. But it did not matter: he was back, again and again, his practiced, careful preparations on her body, giving her time, waiting, using her with gentle hands and a loving mouth. Minna's eyes were full of tears at his wondrous concern: a boy who cared that much for what she felt. At the end, after their third encounter, she was ready for her part, her contribution to their pleasure. Their union was simultaneous and wondrous, an explosion that shook her body like a great wind and left it shaking with the aftershocks of joy.

Exhausted, they lay together, his head in the crook of her arm, his hand on her breast. 'That was lovely. Fine. You are lovely. You were fine. I feel great.' There was a long silence. Minna savored his presence and the magnificent jolt into the past she had just experienced. Lowell stared into the dark and thought of his luck. Then he said, to cover the oppressive silence, 'Tell me about some of the other papers you heard.'   'Are you serious?'   'I'm serious. If I can't go with you, I'd like to hear what went on.'   'Well, someone gave a paper on the Cardiff Giant, who now resides in Iowa. Have you ever heard about him?'   'Never.'   'Well, he was said to have been discovered on a farm in upstate New York, in the town of Cardiff, in 1869. It was an enormous stone figure of a man and was said by the first witnesses to be a petrified man from biblical times. He was ten feet long and weighed over three thousand pounds. Some smart promoters took the figure to Syracuse, to Albany, and to Boston and charged thousands of people one dollar apiece to view it. Over the figure they strung a banner that read, "GENESIS 6:4. THERE WERE GIANTS IN THE EARTH IN THOSE DAYS." After the promoters had made a fortune, a nosy scientist discovered that the giant was made of pure Iowa gypsum, and then it was revealed that the promoters had secretly buried him on that farm. But a faithful believer in the giant, convinced it was not a hoax, brought him back here and stored him in a warehouse. In 1934, someone got it out and exhibited it at a state fair.'   'I wish I'd been around to see it. Where is he now?'   'Somewhere around here, lying in state as a permanent exhibit in some private museum in Iowa, I forget where. So you can still see him, if you want.' Lowell turned on his side and put his head on her breast. She played with his hair, arranging it behind his ear. He said, 'You're full of good stories.'   'I'm a historian. That's what history is, in the main.'   'I thought it was a collection of verifiable facts, with some interpretation thrown in.'   'So far as fact can be rescued from a past that is overlaid with human fiction and forgetfulness, it is fact. In that way frauds, bizarre events and curiosities are interesting. They start as accepted fact and usually turn out to be invention and hoax that somehow have seeped into the official record. Some of them survive as fact, some of them are revealed to be fraud, like the Cardiff Giant. Pure but lovely fake, in the cause of theological evidence.' Lowell was silent. Minna thought he was thinking about the unreliability of history. But he said, 'Could we do it again?'   'Not tonight, my fine fellow. I'm tired. You'd better get dressed and move your jalopy from the front of the building.'   'I hate to go. I like it here, in this bed, lying with you.'   'I love having you here, but there is the maid who arrives early and . . . and . . . the disparity. What would be said of me?'   'And of me.'   'No, you're safe enough. But I would be—some monstrosity, when they talked about us.' Lowell laughed. In the near-dark Minna was moved by the charm of his face when he smiled. When his smile expanded into his light, lovely laugh, she wanted to say something wantonly endearing to him. But she held back, reminding herself that this was an impossible, ludicrous, incongruous love. She moved into a safer mode of discourse. 'Mark Twain once said, "The very ink with which all history is written is merely fluid prejudice." My friend Liz Becker used to quote this to me.'   'The photographer? You know her?'   'Yes, we were roommates in college. Do you know her work?'   'I saw an exhibit in Des Moines of her pictures, showing retarded kids dancing in a field, fat idiot twins with jug ears, and Korean veterans with no arms and legs. Hard stuff to look at for very long.'   'Yes, I suppose so, but there's a pride in those people, a sense of the way they value themselves.'   'I suppose so.'   'Get up, Lowell, my love.   'I am. I am getting up.'

He turned on the bed light. Minna watched him dress, loving every jerky, boylike movement, every swift turn of his head. He bent over to kiss her. She wrapped her arm around his head to pull him down and kissed him hard. 'Tomorrow?' she asked when she could breathe again.   He said, 'There's a good revival at the Bijou, *Tell Me That You Love Me, Junie Moon*. Liza Minnelli is in it. Want to see it—with me?'   Minna laughed. 'What a curious title. No, I think not. But you go, and come by later and tell me about it. What is tomorrow, Friday?'   'Yes, all day,' he said, and smiled.   'Fine,' she said. As he lifted the chain latch, she suddenly, stupidly, was moved to ask, 'Lowell, tell me, have you ever heard of the kidnapping of the Lindbergh baby?'   'No, what was that about?'   'How about Gertrude Ederle? Do you know who she is?'   'Nope. Who is she? What is this? Twenty Questions or something?'   'No, I just wondered. I'm still thinking about history. Pretty ancient history by now. The olden times.'   He said, 'Good night,' and she said, 'Good night. Tomorrow,' and turned out the light.

Alone, again in the dark, Minna stretched, pulled the blankets to her chin and lay still on her back, her arms folded beneath her head. 'How old am I now? Seventeen,

I believe. I have retreated to that age, psychically, physically. I am full of young desire, wet between my legs. Filled with pleasure at my body—and his. It's all real, I am an old fool, but I believe it is all real. I am the Cardiff Giant of Iowa history, an ancient gypsum figure passing myself off as Aphrodite, a pure, happy hoax. God help me.'

Lowell sat in Pete's having lunch with his roommate, Ivan Horn. Lowell started to talk, and went on and on. Horn asked him, 'When are you going to shut up and let me say something?' But Lowell was deaf to anything but his own lyricism. 'She's golden. Her hair, the little hairs on her arms are yellow and delicate. I've never seen a grown woman so, so elegant and yet so warm and well, lush, I suppose that's the word. Back east she's a full professor with tenure and all that, but with me she's not like that. She's . . . she's . . . I don't know, loving and gentle and her lust is as sweet and great as mine. Sometimes I think even greater.'   'How old *is* she?'   'I have no idea. I never asked her. I don't want to know, I guess. Much older than I am, I suppose. She had a son who fought in Vietnam. He died after that, I don't know how old he was. But what difference does it make? She's great, she likes making love, she's got soft hands. When I'm there, it's like I'm with a girl, a beautiful girl. She's good to me.'

Ivan tried to ask more identifying questions, but Lowell would only answer with elaborate myths of womanly beauty and fanciful accounts about his new discovery of the mysteries of love. He talked on, telling Ivan of his adoration. He detailed some of what they did together, what she offered him and what he gave her in return. He described a dialogue of love and service, passion and retribution. On and on he went until Ivan became bored by Lowell's wild, romantic narrative. 'Where does all this take place? Who is she?

What's her name? How old is she, really? What's wrong with telling me?' Lowell said, 'No. It's a secret, she's very private. I don't believe my luck and I don't want to spoil it.' 'I don't believe you,' said Ivan, thinking he might anger Lowell into revealing something. 'It's all made up. Why would a beautiful woman professor want *you?*' 'I don't know. I don't understand that any more than you do.' 'It's all bunk. You're full of bull. You're having fantasies, daydreams. You're sick, fella.' Lowell smiled at Ivan, and picked up his check and his books. 'You're probably right. I don't believe it myself. But that's the way it is.'

November 28, 1978. 'Dear Minna: I was very glad to have your letter. I have been thinking of you out there in Iowa and yes, you are right. I have a vision of fields full of brown cornstalks, snow-encrusted pigs and a horizon that stretches everlastingly in every direction. I have now readjusted my interior lenses, even my preconceived negatives. I now picture you, still in your elegant clothes (do you still have *furs?*) and mink-topped boots hiking up a snowy Iowa City incline to meet your students at the summit.

'You write of your new "unsuitable and unnatural youth." Well, it may seem so to you, not to me. It is a commonplace of everyone's experience, I am sure, that one's friends always remain the age and shape they were in the time you were most together. Perhaps it is because we have not seen much of each other since that last year at college, that it comes as no surprise at all to me to hear that you are still young. I never thought of you as aging at all.

'Maud, of course, is frozen in time for me. Even if she had lived, my recording eye remembers her in only one way, in her bed with the pongee spread pulled up over her big self on that afternoon after Luther had left her room and we had just come back from photographing—who? I don't remember who. Even the sight of her coffin in that church in Ravena cannot erase that memory, set in some kind of eternal aspic. Why is it that in all the time we lived together, I never photographed her (or you, for that matter)? Every time a biographer or writer comes by, I regret the omission publicly, but privately I rejoice, because that memory would have been wiped out by the photograph. I want one view of her: covered up on that narrow Barnard bed, for once without those distorting glasses, and a new, knowing little smile on her face.

'I have been distracted from writing that your youth is not unnatural to me. I envy your finding love, a boy with the fine, poetic name. I hope all your evident pleasure goes on for a long time, a very long time. Forever, I almost wrote, but of course, not forever. The odds are never very good for an enduring relationship of any sort, let alone this one. Enjoy it while you can. How great it must be to have something so good now that you might have expected only at the start. Relish your illusion of being young. I used to have a dream, a queer one, that I found myself growing younger by the moment. I could see the changes in my face, my body. The spots and wrinkles left my hands, like a film running backward. But I always woke up before the regression stopped. I never have that dream now. Reality has invaded even my sleep.

'Some small personal news: I have a new exhibit at the House of Photography in Manhattan. Hilton Kramer, who is now very taken with photography, was complimentary in the *Times*. A few other reviews were effusive and so, naturally, gratifying. All the signed prints were sold the first evening, which augurs well for the book Aperture will publish next spring. So it goes, in that department of my life.

'The sad news is that in July Helene returned to Kings County Hospital to be told she had a recurrence of her cancer. We thought she was safe, had beaten the odds, but then, who ever beats mortality? Her second breast was removed, but there was evidence that the cancer had spread to her lymph nodes. She stood the second operation well, considering that she is almost seventy and radical surgery is not simple at her age. In a few weeks she was back home. Since then we have had four extraordinary months together. With the heavy sense of fatality hanging over us, we were able to renew physical and psychic ties I thought had been worn out in the more than thirty-eight years we have lived and loved together. She jokes about her new, flat-chested physique, saying she is now the boy she had always felt she would like to be. The scars are dreadful, but I forget them when I lie close to her, luxuriating in her brave and humorous person.

'The prognosis is poor, we both know that, even the time we have is in deep shadow. So we are now living a kind of crammed, charged, encapsulated life with each other. We feel suspended in time and space, we are re-creating an unnatural youth, as you say. And as with youth, we know it will pass quickly. Quality of time and love has been offered us, not quantity.

'Thank you for the postcard. I had not seen the giantess photograph. I love it, especially the rapacious hooded vulture look in her eyes, as if she were about to consume all the lesser, shorter mortals around her. . . . Write when you can, and remember us in your prayers, if you have some good ones. I have none, but every now and then I shut my eyes and ask the powers that be to be kind to Helene. Beyond that, I don't know much to ask for. Love, Liz'

Every Sunday morning Richard telephoned Minna. 'How are you?'   'Fine,' she said. 'How are *you?*'   'Oh, very good. I miss you. How's the new car doing?'   'Very well.

It's a great car, but it's cold here now so the top has to be up all the time. Even with it up, the canvas doesn't keep out the cold.' There was a long silence, and then Richard asked, 'What do you think of that supersonic plane that went from New York to Paris in three hours, and goes regularly?' 'Amazing.' 'We ought to plan a vacation to France on it, maybe over New Year's. What do you think?' Minna was silent. 'I may not be back by then.' 'What? Why not? When does the semester end?' 'Before Christmas, but there's other things, the research I am in the middle of. . . . ' Richard said nothing. Then he said, 'It's a season of disasters, isn't it, first the flood in India that now is said to have killed thousands, and then the earthquake in Iran. Twenty-five thousand died, the *Times* says.' 'Yes, we get the *Times* here every afternoon. Even out here.' 'Oh, of course.' 'Have you seen *The Deer Hunter* yet?' Minna asked. 'No. Why? Is it good?' 'Not very, but it made me think of Grant. I could hardly sit through it.' 'I avoid war movies,' said Richard in a dry voice. 'Well, when can I expect you home?' 'I don't know, Richard.' '*Are* you coming back, Minna? Is that what you're trying to tell me? 'I just don't know.' 'I see. Well, good-bye. Do you want me to call you next Sunday?' 'If you wish. Good-bye.' 'Good-bye,' he said, and hung up.

Minna dressed for her luncheon appointment with a new acquaintance, the painter Lester Dickens, whom she had met the week before at a dinner party. Her closet was filled with proper skirts, blouses and dresses. These she pushed aside to reach the twice-washed blue jeans that hung at the back. She kicked against the bottle of gin on the floor, sending it farther back against her row of shoes. 'Good shot,' she said to herself. Hanging over the blue jeans was a heavy wool turtleneck sweater. She put it and the jeans on, and pulled on her leather boots, which laced up the sides. Her Eskimo jacket with its warm fur hood was hard to maneuver over the sweater but she managed it. With scarf and fur mittens she felt like some small child being sent out into the snow bundled up so tightly she could barely move. 'All I need is clips to hold my mittens on to my sleeves,' she thought. When she was ready to leave she reviewed herself in the bathroom floor-length mirror. She saw, as if by X ray, her twenty-year-old self, slender and delicate-looking within the layers of clothing, straight and vigorous. There was no extra flesh, she imagined, her arms and legs had their old languorous curves, the skin on her face was devoid of the marks of age or weather, her eyes were very bright. She smiled at her image: her mouth still curved tenderly, in the old way. What she saw, she understood, was what she remembered, what she believed existed under the heavy winter clothing, what Lowell had persuaded her he saw. Only her hair. She smiled at herself and looked closely, understanding why his vision failed him. Strands of her hair escaped the hood. It was not Lowell's night-blinded, love-besotted light blond, but white. *'Sein und Schlein,'* she told herself, and went out, slamming the door behind her.

Lester Dickens ordered a large pizza and two beers for them. Angelo's was a favorite eating place for students and rushed teachers. It offered three choices of food, but pizza was its specialty. Lester, a heavyset fellow with a protruding belly and a cheerful, homey, uncomplicated face, had intrigued Minna at dinner one evening with his talk about circuses. He in turn had silently admired her sparkle, her luminous, interested blue eyes, her slender liveliness 'at her age,' as he put it to his daughter when he got home. 'She must be sixty or so. Yet she has the grace and movements of a young woman. Something uncommon about that. Even odd.' His daughter had looked puzzled and unconvinced.

Minna looked at her watch. 'I thought this was to be an instant pizza.'   'Nothing is that fast at lunchtime in Iowa City. Do you have a class or something?'   'No, but I want to get to the pool for my daily workout. I overslept this morning.' Lester watched Minna doodling on her napkin with a ballpoint pen. Her drawing was unusually regular, he thought, and in perspective. She was covering the rectangular paper with steps, the treads colored in, the risers carefully striated up and down. While she doodled, she asked him to tell her about his circus paintings. 'I've been mad for circuses all my life, boy and man, and now in middle age, my passion for them is even greater. I go whenever there is one within three hundred miles. My preference is for the small traveling circuses with sideshows. By now I know many of the performers, animals, the wonders and oddities. I've painted many of them, the half-man/half-woman, a sword-swallower, a snake charmer, a contortionist.'   'I've seen those paintings at the museum. Strange, isn't it, how we feel such sympathy for what a friend of mine calls "singular people?" '   'I often think about that. A bear by itself is not interesting to me, but a performing bear, centered in a spotlight, all four feet planted on a small ball, muzzle pointed into the air, incredibly poised: *that* is something. It's as if his presence were raised to a special height. He is reaching beyond his animal self, to the act.'   'Yes, I like that. It's the same, I suppose, with the eccentrics of the world. We, the onlookers, the painters, and photographers, are commonplace and ordinary. The fat lady, the midget, the giant, they are the exceptional departures. We are cold and contained, they are full of the passion of their differences, on proud display. They give it away in their acts, too.'   Lester said there was something in that. 'Everything in the circus is stretched and charged. Nothing is real. Normal life is scorned, really, at every turn. The lights, the round formation of every act, the tinny music and drums, the clowns making fun of the acts, of themselves. For me there is a heightened sense of idyllic, innocent life. I love it. I'm never bored when the acts are poor, only full of sympathy. I breathe faster, my heart beats hard. And later, when I am in my studio painting the sounds, the lights, the people and animals, I feel the same way.'

Minna said, 'When I was in college I used to go with a friend to a place in New York, a Forty-second Street basement under a penny arcade. Hubert's, it was called. Downstairs there were sideshow freaks. I thought they were wonderful, monarchs in a kingdom of one—proud, aloof people who would never talk to us, or even look at us. They allowed my friend to photograph them because it was proper, fitting, for the special people they were, to have a photograph taken. They must have led bleak lives, but there was a kind of childlike cheerfulness about all of them.'

The pizza and beers arrived. They began to eat quickly. Lester said, between bites, 'You seem to like Iowa City. You look wonderful in those student clothes. Are you as happy as you look?'   'Yes, I'm foolishly happy, in a way I can't believe. Like an adolescent girl.' And then, as she wiped her fingers and finished her beer, she said, surprising herself as she spoke, 'I'm in love. Isn't that absurd?'   '*Well*,' said Lester, offering her another napkin from the container on the table, and taking a handful himself. 'That's something. I haven't fallen in love since I was almost thirty and met my wife-to-be in art school. How did you manage to do that?'   Minna, confounded by what she had revealed, laughed and said, 'It's an illusion, I'm sure. Like the girl who is sawed in two by a magician onstage. Nothing more. Self-delusion and audience decep-

tion. Forget I said that, will you, please?'   'Okay. But
how I envy you. Even if it is an illusion. Some valuable
things are invented by belief. I haven't even had the illusion
I was in love for so long. You look at if you—felt fine about
it.'   'I do. But that's all there is to it.'   'Yes, I'll
remember.' They figured their checks, gathered up their
belongings. From the pile of soiled napkins, Lester pulled
one out. 'Is this your usual doodle?' he asked.   Minna
looked at it. 'Yes, I guess so. I always draw stairs. It's about
all I know how to do.'   'Do you start from the bottom
and draw up, or from the top?'   'I start from the top.
What does that mean?'   'No idea,' said Lester. He took
the checks and their money and pushed Minna through the
line of waiting students. 'I enjoyed that,' he said as they
stood on College Avenue, buttoning their jackets. Minna
wound her scarf around her neck, and agreed. 'We'll do it
again,' he said.   'Indeed we will. And, Lester, add me
to your list of interesting freaks.'   'I will. I'll put you
in a painting if you like.' They both laughed, at nothing
in particular, and went their separate ways on the street.

In the middle of December the weather turned hostile. Wind
from the river tore through the wide streets. Snow fell
sporadically, freezing like treacherous piecrust along the
edges of the streets. At once, new, clean snow fell to cover
it. Ice frosted the top of the snow. Minna had not moved
Maud since the night she had left it in the parking lot across
from the Joint. She worried about denting the shining new
fenders or being collided with on the hazardous streets.
Lowell suggested he meet her wherever she was in the evening and drive her home. He knew she was afraid of the
ice on the streets. Minna had never known such cold, such
unremitting snow and ice. With very little warning, the
kitten had turned tiger. The gentle, humane landscape of

southern Iowa had become threatening, frightening, untamed and wild. Minna's every move, day or evening, was ruled by the weather.

One Friday evening, under cover of the early dark and cloud-burdened black skies, Minna and Lowell went on foot through heavy snow to the Hamburg Inn. At the door of Schaeffer Hall she had taken his arm. He responded to her concern about the footing by holding her hand firmly in his. Because of the bad weather, the popular place was almost empty. They found a booth, shed their layers of jackets and sweaters and ordered chicken, biscuits and gravy, 'the house specialty,' Lowell advised her. In the booth he found a dog-eared copy of Friday's *Des Moines Register*. While they waited for their food, Lowell read the funnies to her. He was good at accents and dialects. Minna laughed at and with him. He was a boy, she thought, with a boy's fondness for *Peanuts* and *Pogo*. When he had fully explored the page for his favorite strips and their political and social implications, which he explained to Minna, he moved on to the sports page. He lectured to her on the scores of last Sunday's professional games and Saturday's college football, especially the excellence of the Iowa Hawkeyes, to whom he was devoted. With his usual humor he commented on quarterbacks' skill or lack of it and the proficiency of the 'wide receivers' and the 'tight ends.' These were terms Minna had never heard before. To her mind, emptied of everything these days but the enormous love for him that flooded it, the unfamiliar vocabulary of the funnies and football rang with the music of lyric poetry. Her standards of intellectual conversation, raised and strengthened in her years as an academic wife of a doctor, relaxed and sank contentedly into Lowell's preferred areas of thought. During the weeks she had known him, she found herself directing her attention down instead of the usual straining upward. This lack of intellectual effort, the wit with which he infused all his popular interests, made her feel, for the first time in her adult life, easy and comfortable. She was Lowell's peer, no more. She enjoyed every moment of his smiling dissertation on the merits of the Green Bay Packers, his favorite team. Especially did she enjoy his smile.

When the chicken dinner arrived, Lowell grew silent. They ate without speaking, looking occasionally at each other and smiling when their eyes met. Minna surmised that Lowell was gathering his courage to ask her something. She waited, trying to take small bites of the gravy-covered mashed potatoes she had always disliked. When it came, it was not a question but a demand: 'Tell me something about your life. You know about mine, almost day by day.'   'There's less of yours to know. Mine might take all night.'   'What questions does he want answered,' she wondered, by his indirection. This is what Yeats meant when he said, "Love is the crooked thing." When were you in grade school? When was your son born? How long have you been married? How long have you taught? Nothing in autobiography was without its calendar milestones.' When she was silent, Lowell scraped a piece of roll into the remains of gravy and cleaned his plate. 'This is very good. Don't you think so?'   'I do, but I'm not very hungry. Have mine.'   'Thanks, I will.' He asked the waitress for another glass of milk and Minna ordered black coffee. Lowell said, 'It's nice to be waited on for a change, and then he asked, 'Minna, what was your college year?' Minna looked at him stonily. Here it was, at last, his curiosity breaking through his blinded, unquestioning myopia, in the form of a direct question. She said, 'What you are really asking is how old I am. Isn't that right, Lowell?' He blushed and stared down at his milk. 'I guess I am curious, yes. But I know it's none of my damned business.'   'How old do you think I am?' Lowell appeared to be making elaborate, silent calculations as he looked at her. He said, 'Somewhere around forty, maybe.' Minna smiled. She saw that forty to this boy was old. Adding twenty years to his vague figure would not make her, in his eyes, much older than that. How old was Grant really when he died? Somewhere around fourteen psychically, no more. But she found she could not bear to philosophize or lie to this boy she loved. 'Somewhere around there,' she said, 'but higher rather than lower.' He looked troubled, as though he was angry at himself for having questioned her. He pushed the check toward her. 'I don't get paid until tomorrow. I'll pay you back.'   'No problem,' she said, picking it up. 'Are you coming back with me?'   'Sure. Of course I'm coming back. What did you think?'

That night, because of the snow, and because the next day was Saturday, Lowell did not get up afterward and go back to his apartment. They slept together tenderly, like orphans of the storm who curled into each other for warmth, comfort and sympathy. In the morning, they woke late and felt refreshed. They went downstairs to the cafeteria for breakfast. Lowell ate an enormous meal while Minna, too content to eat, drank orange juice and black coffee. It was still snowing. They sat near the window and watched the black Iowa River make its way through pure white banks. A pair of mallard ducks hunkered down connubially near the edge, bleakly eyeing the inhospitable landscape. 'It's not even good weather for ducks,' Lowell said. 'I'm working lunch today. I'd better get going. I hope the car starts and the brakes don't freeze up on me.'   'Do you work tonight?'   'Usually. But I've got to go to the library to work on my term paper.'   'I'm meeting my students at the Joint for a farewell end-of-term party. The Joint of all places, but they chose it. Do you want to come by and pick me up when it's over?'   'I do. What time?'   'About

ten? I'll wait for you at the door.'   'Fine. I'll be there.'
He smiled his sweet smile, swallowed so hard that his Ad-
am's apple moved in his thin neck, and whispered, 'My
love.' They were both silent. Lowell said, to change the
subject and break the heavy silence, 'They say the snow will
stop this afternoon.' They smiled at each other, he leaned
over and whispered, 'I love you.' She said, in a whisper, 'I
love you, too.' He stood up, reached over to the next table
and picked up an abandoned *Register*. 'Got to see what Pogo
did today,' he said. He turned back and waved to Minna
at the door. She sat finishing her coffee and watching the
cold mallards try to pick their way along the bank in the
high snow. 'Around forty,' she thought. 'Perhaps even
younger. I feel immortal. It might be that I am.'

Minna said good night and good-bye to her students. With
some effort she pushed open the door of the Joint, against
the wind she could feel blowing hard. It was a quarter to
ten, but sitting there with her beer she suddenly decided
she wanted to start her car in the parking lot across the
street. If Maud responded, she would follow Lowell in her
car to Iowa House. She had found she felt less confined by
the weather when her car was not too far away. As the door
shut behind her she could hear the laughter of students at
the tables, and the townies at the bar. The snow still fell,
soft and heavy, heaped into airy shapes. She was surrounded
by dwarfed presences: bushes, fences, bicycles, whitened
and almost unrecognizable. 'Pray Maud will not be frozen
stiff,' Minna thought as she came to the curb, picking her
way with care. 'And that I can find her.'
   She pushed herself against the wind, her eyes almost shut
by the blowing wind and snow. She stepped over the hump-
backed ice barrier into the street; her head was down. Her
eyes were fixed on her perilous footing. She never saw the

snow-whitened car coming fast into the entrance to the parking lot. In one brilliant flash that illuminated mounds of sparkling snow, she felt the mortal impact of steel against bone. At once, she was freed, from pain and loss, from the heat and contagion of love. She descended through the inverted cellar doors and struck off across the Channel that ran through the dark. Fearless, blind, then deaf, she entered the infinite blackness where all passions are extinguished. For Minna it was the final irony.

<hr/>

RICHARD ROMAN TELEPHONED LIZ to tell her about Minna's death. Liz offered him the stock condolences. He said there would be a memorial service for Minna at the Ethical Culture Society in two weeks. He hoped she would come. She said she would, and put the receiver down quietly on its hook. She sat on the small stool they kept near the telephone for extended calls, thinking she ought to go upstairs to tell Helene. Then she decided not to interrupt her sleep: she had been awake with pain most of the night.

Liz slipped off the stool onto the braided rug. For a long moment she made no move, and then she bent her legs into the lotus position. 'Minna, so perfectly made, so well suited, it seemed, to the demands of the world, so socially successful. Professor of manners, history, love. I thought she was destined to go on forever, from one graceful, ageless accommodation to the next. Unlike that unsightly genius Maud, who left the party early.' Staring at the rug's circular pattern, Liz thought of the evening the three of them, putting off the cleaning chore, had stood with their arms around each other.

'I'm here,' Liz thought. 'The one left. Odd woman out. Or in. Still afloat, still kicking. Minna would like that image. Endurance is like effort, I suppose. It counts for something.' Suddenly she stood up and raised her arms to put them around the long-gone Maud and the newly dead Minna. She felt them press their unsubstantial arms across her back. 'All right,' she said aloud. 'Let's get on with it, before the dark sets in,' and started upstairs.

CPSIA information can be obtained
at www.ICGtesting.com
Printed in the USA
BVHW041705081122
651458BV00016B/217